THE VAMPIRE'S LAST DANCE

WITCH ISLAND BRIDES, BOOK 1

DEANNA CHASE

BAYOU MOON PUBLISHING

Copyright © 2018 by Deanna Chase

First Edition 2018

Cover Art by Renee George

Editing by Angie Ramey

ISBN: 978-1-940299-57-0

All rights reserved. No part of this publication may be reproduced, stored in, or introduced into a retrieval system, or transmitted in any form, or by any means (electronic, mechanical, photocopying, recording, or otherwise) without the prior written permission of both the copyright owner and the publisher of this book.

This book is a work of fiction. Names, characters, places, and incidents are products of the author's imagination or are used fictitiously. Any resemblance to actual events, locals, business establishments, or persons, living or dead, are entirely coincidental.

Bayou Moon Press, LLC

ABOUT THIS BOOK

Welcome to Love Spells, the line of paranormal books where every happily-ever-after comes with a big dose of laughter.

The Vampire's Last Dance (Witch Island Brides, Book 1)

She's a witch who carries a family curse, destined to never get her happily ever after. Felicia Patterson has come to terms with the fact that she'll never get to be with her one true love... whoever he happens to be. But when the sexiest vampire she's ever seen walks onto Witch Island, she can't help her fluttering heart.

He's a vampire who's been burned before, destined to never love again. Christoph Parks has sworn off relationships. In the century that he's walked the earth, he's only known heartbreak and disappointment. But one smile from the island's sassy florist has his icy heart melting. And now that the pair have been thrown together to save their loved ones' wedding from imploding, can they also overcome a brutal curse, find a way to trust, and finally get the love that they deserve?

CHAPTER 1

When Felicia Patterson decided to become a florist, she had no idea she'd end up working with dildos. But here she was, clutching a giant, sparkly pink Jack Rabbit and trying to secure it to a bouquet of greenery while the most gorgeous man she'd ever laid eyes on stared at her with one eyebrow raised.

"Um, hello," Felicia said, heat climbing up her neck and settling into her cheeks. *Good goddess,* she thought as she took in his perfectly chiseled jaw, wideset steel-blue eyes, and his mouth-watering five o'clock shadow. She glanced at the clock. It wasn't even noon yet. Her mouth instantly went dry as she imagined what he might look like once the sun went down.

"Nice bush," he said, nodding to the bouquet of cushion poms she held in her hand.

She glanced down at the obscene sex toy in her

right hand and the foliage clutched in her left. There was no stopping the bubble of laughter that escaped her lips. "They're for a bachelorette party. Custom ordered by the bride. All I have to do is figure out how to attach Mr. Happy to the *bush* and then my day will be complete."

"I bet you say that to all the guys," he said with a wink. "Need some help?"

"Sure." Oh, he was a fun one, wasn't he? Because she couldn't resist, she handed the vibrator to him and then spread the foliage so he could see where the base of the vibrator was supposed to attach to the bouquet.

"Can't say I have much experience in this department, but let's see what we can do." Without hesitation, he palmed the dildo and went to work on inserting it into the bush—ah bouquet.

"I bet a man like you has had plenty of experience." Felicia laughed again, and when he gave her a wicked grin, everything inside her heated. She sucked in a breath and told herself, *Calm down, girl. He's just a man. An extremely sexy one, but still, he's just a man.*

It wasn't like Witch Island didn't have a steady sea of men parading through on a regular basis. The island was *the* place to hold paranormal weddings. The entire community revolved around the constant festivities, and that meant the island hosted new groomsmen pretty much weekly. There was no shortage of weekend flings... if one was looking for that. Felicia hadn't been one to take part in such activities, but as she stared at the man in front of her, she suddenly had a change of heart. What harm could come from enjoying a night or two with a handsome stranger? It wasn't like she was attached to anyone. Esmerelda has seen to that years ago.

Felicia bit back a scowl and swallowed the familiar resentment. She didn't like to be reminded of the curse her cousin had cast over her. The jealous cow. Well, she wasn't here now, was she? And the curse couldn't stop her from enjoying herself for a few days while this sexy man who made her laugh was in town. Just as long as he wasn't the groom.

Please don't let him be the groom.

Once he had the vibrator inserted into the holder she'd fashioned, Felicia used a white silk ribbon to secure it in place. "Perfect," she said, holding the bouquet up to show him their handiwork. "Hopefully the customer likes it. This design was a new one for me."

"Let me guess, Bianca?"

She eyed him with suspicion. If he was marrying Bianca, she was going to need a very large drink. "How'd you know?"

His lips twitched into that wicked smile again, revealing just a hint of his fangs. "She always did have a wild streak."

Vampire. Of course. It wasn't that vampires couldn't go into the sun. They could, it was just that they were sensitive to the light, and all of them at some point passed out during the day and rose again sometime between dusk and evening. It appeared this one had better stamina than most. Time to find out if she needed to polish off her flirting skills or if she was doomed for a pity party. "*Do not* tell me you're the groom. Good goddess, if she finds out you helped with these, heads will roll. The groom is not supposed to be privy to bachelorette party details."

"You're safe," he said, holding out a hand. "Christoph Parks, the best man."

"Oh, the best man." Relief rushed through her, and she gazed up at him with renewed interest. "Well in that case, welcome to Witch Island. I'm Felicia." She reached to shake his hand but belatedly realized the hand she offered was still holding the dildo bouquet. She immediately dropped it. The bouquet hit the counter and rolled, landing on the floor. A loud buzzing noise sounded from the bouquet as the entire thing vibrated. "Holy goddess. Did that just happen?"

Christoph let out a full-throated laugh as he calmly plucked the bouquet up off the floor and deftly turned the vibrator off. Without missing a beat, he clasped her hand and said, "It certainly has been my pleasure to meet you, Miss Felicia."

Just then, two of the island's older witches strode in. They were sisters, but couldn't be more different if they tried. One, Mary Ellen, had her gray hair piled on her head, a few strands of her long, perfect curls framing her face. The other, Quincy, swept her long, beautiful silver mane over one shoulder and glanced around. Quincy's gaze landed on Christoph. Her thin lips spread into a wide, interested smile, but as she focused on the bouquet, she frowned. "You do know that's not how that works, right, sweetie? Because that would really ruin the fantasy that's taking shape in my mind right this moment."

Christoph frowned. "What?"

"That sparkly pink dildo should be poking into the bush, not out of it."

"Quincy!" Mary Ellen exclaimed, one gloved hand covering her mouth. "You're terrible."

She shrugged. "I just want to make sure this handsome piece of man-meat understands how these things work. Because if he doesn't, that's a crime against humanity."

"I think I've got it covered." He winked at Felicia, and her knees went a little weak.

"Tell me, handsome," Quincy said, placing her hand on his arm. "Are you here to get married this weekend? Because if you are, I might just have to give your bride a run for her money."

"Definitely not," he said, shaking his head. "Just here to make sure my brother makes it down the aisle."

"Oh, good." Quincy turned to her sister. "I haven't seen anyone this delicious since that shifter came to town last year. What was his name, Mary Ellen?"

"Raven Black."

"Right. He went by Rave. He had such large hands. I never did get a chance to find out if what they say about size is true." She pumped her eyebrows and glanced from Christoph's hands to his crotch. "Looks like you have big, strong hands. Do you have plans this evening?"

Christoph took a small step back, clearly surprised by the woman's boldness. His gaze landed on Felicia, and she had to swallow a laugh at the faint trace of panic in his eyes. "Um, actually," he said, turning back to Quincy, "I do have plans. You see, just before you walked in, I asked Felicia if she'd join me for dinner and a midnight stroll."

Quincy turned cold eyes on Felicia. The look was so icy, Felicia actually shivered. "You don't want to date her, gorgeous. She doesn't have the best of luck with men."

What the hell? Oh no, she didn't just go there. It was on. Usually Felicia tolerated Quincy's aggressive brand of banter, but now she was just being mean. The florist stepped around the counter and linked her arm through Christoph's. She gave Quincy a sickly sweet smile and said, "He was really impressed with my ability to handle the Jack Rabbit. Better luck next time, Q."

"No surprise there, considering you can't hold a man long enough for a second date," Quincy said dryly. Then she turned on her heel and strode to the door. "You coming, Mary Ellen?"

"No," her sister said, crossing her arms over her chest. "I came in for some fresh flowers and I'll be getting them, thank you very much. I'll just see you back at home. Try to shake off that bitchy attitude before I get there or forget about the happy cupcakes I was gonna bake."

"You wouldn't," Quincy said, glaring.

"I would. You're being downright rude."

Quincy huffed, and without another word, she disappeared out into the village streets.

Mary Ellen turned to Felicia. "I'm really sorry about that. She turns really surly when she hasn't gotten… um"—her cheeks turned bright red as she cleared her throat—"enough male attention."

"Of course," Felicia said, trying to be sympathetic. But all she could think about was the fact that *she* hadn't dated anyone in over a decade and she still hadn't turned into a raving witch.

"Perhaps she could use one of these," Christoph said, holding up the vibrator bouquet.

Mary Ellen laughed. "You know, dear, I think you're right. Maybe I'll order her something online."

"I have the perfect website for you," Felicia said as she fished out a business card. As she handed it to Mary Ellen, she added, "They have great prices and service. Lots of options, too."

"Perfect. Now, about those fresh flowers…"

Five minutes later, Mary Ellen was humming to herself as she walked out of the shop, a bouquet of spring flowers tucked under her arm.

Christoph eyed Felicia.

She pushed back her dark hair, suddenly self-conscious. Had she even put makeup on that morning? Just a little brown eyeliner and mascara to highlight her blue eyes. She prayed it wasn't running down her face.

"So… you're a sexpert?" he asked.

She sputtered. "Excuse me?"

He gestured to the vibrator bouquet. "You seem to have some knowledge."

"I… uh, know things," she said, laughing. "Why? Do you need some lessons?"

A predatory grin spread over his face as he shook his head. Then he scanned her from head to toe, his hungry gaze once again heating her from the inside out. "Lessons aren't necessary, but I'm always up for learning new tricks."

"Well, aren't you the forward one," Felicia said, amused and feeling bold. "In that case, why don't you take me out to dinner tonight for real, and we'll see what kind of trouble we can get into?"

His predatory smile vanished, replaced by a pleased one. "Eight o'clock?"

Butterflies took over in her stomach as she suddenly became very nervous about what he might expect from her, but she pasted on a smile and nodded. She wasn't going to let herself chicken out of a fun weekend with the hottest guy she'd ever met. A girl had to live sometimes, didn't she? "Sounds perfect. You can pick me up here."

"It's a date. See you then, sexpert Felicia." He headed for the door. But just before he reached the handle, he turned back around. "I um, better grab those bouquets or Bianca is going to have my head on a platter."

Felicia started gathering the half-dozen vibrator bouquets. "I was wondering why you'd stopped in here. I didn't imagine it was *just* to flirt with me."

"If I'd known the florist was this much fun, I'd have stopped in here two days ago when I got into town." He pulled out a credit card and tapped it on the counter.

"We'll just have to make up for lost time." She took his credit card. "I assume you're paying the balance?"

"He most definitely is," Bianca said from the store doorway. The tall, ethereal blond beauty strode into the shop, her movements as graceful as a runway model. "My bestie just loves a good party, don't you, Christoph?" She slid her arm through his and patted his chest. "This is his present to me." Her gaze landed on the bouquets and the pretty blonde threw her head back and laughed. "Oh my god, those are perfect."

Felicia smiled, pleased with herself. She prided herself on going the extra mile to make every bride not just happy, but thrilled. It didn't always work out, but it looked like this time she'd hit her mark dead center… so to speak. "I'm so glad you like them."

"Like them?" Her eyes widened. "I love them. And any woman who has the sense of humor to make them look like they are poking out of a bush is a woman I want to hang out with. Please come to the bachelorette party tonight. It's going to be off the hook. We've got a table reserved at Witchin' Impossible. The boys from down under are putting on a show for us."

Christoph cleared his throat. "Sorry, Bianca. She has plans."

"With who? You?" She giggled, tapping her red-stained lips. "Not anymore. Not tonight anyway. Tonight is all about girls' night out. No boys allowed. At least not any who aren't shaking their groove things." She turned to Felicia. "Right?"

Felicia glanced between them. The stormy look in Christoph's eyes as he glared at Bianca made her shiver. There was a dangerous vibe rolling off him that made her both excited and nervous. Bianca just batted her eyes at him, completely unconcerned. "Um, I..." Felicia started.

"Don't worry about it, Felicia," he said, still staring at Bianca. "How about breakfast? The Sweet Caldron?"

"I'd love to, but I have to work in the morning. The wedding florals still need to be assembled."

He finally turned his intense gaze on her. "I meant breakfast after you watch the boys from down under show off all their goods."

Bianca rolled her eyes.

But Felicia just nodded. There was no way to get out of going to the show she'd already seen a dozen times. It was the go-to bachelorette party destination, and there was just no way to avoid it when friends came to town to get married. Still, she wasn't going to pass up the opportunity to go out with this man. She didn't know what kind of hold this vampire had over her, but at that moment she just didn't care. If he was only on the island for a few days, she wasn't going to let a little thing like respectability get in her way.

"Sure." She handed him her phone. "Put in your number, and I'll text you when the show's over."

He deftly inserted his contact number and when he handed back the phone, he held on to her hand for a moment longer than necessary. Electricity passed between them, and Felicia started mentally counting down the minutes until she would see him again.

CHAPTER 2

"Champagne for everyone!" Bianca stood in the middle of the bachelorette party bus and held up a bottle of Cristal.

Her bridal party instantly produced their champagne flutes, waiting anxiously for them to be filled. When Bianca got to Felicia, the florist held her glass out but didn't take a sip. She didn't want to drink too much before she met up with Christoph later. She didn't want to forget one moment of her time with the beautiful man.

"A toast!" Bianca's maid of honor called. She held up her glass and said, "To the bravest woman I know. Forever is a long-ass time when you're marrying a vampire."

The rest of the party chimed in their agreement, but Bianca just beamed, her eyes lighting up with pure happiness. "When he's the perfect man, ladies, you just know. Forever can't come soon enough."

Felicia's heart swelled. This was why she lived on Witch Island and ran a floral shop that was dedicated to supplying flowers for over a hundred weddings a year. If she couldn't get her own wedding with a happily-ever-after, she would just have to live vicariously through those who were lucky enough to not be cursed to live a solitary life. The familiar ache in her chest was back, the one that always materialized when she was reminded of her plight in life. She'd spent two years in a full-on depression after Esmerelda had taken her revenge. Felicia was done with that. Done with feeling sorry for herself. She'd vowed to live her life to the fullest and to appreciate the love around her even if she was left on the sidelines.

"To Bianca and her loving fiancé," Felicia said, raising her glass.

The bridesmaids echoed her toast, and only then did Felicia allow herself a sip of the delicious champagne. She closed her eyes and licked her lips, savoring the tart flavor.

"Uh-oh," Bianca said with a wink. "Looks like we have someone who loves Cristal just as much as I do." Before Felicia could stop her, Bianca topped off her glass and said, "Drink up, my new friend. Tonight we party!"

Felicia, apparently unable to say no to the gorgeous vampire, did as she was told. The bubbles hit her throat, and when she swallowed they seemed to spread through her body, making her skin tingle. Felicia grinned. Oh goddess. Bianca had gotten the champagne from Tally's, the specialty liquor store where everything was spelled. In this case, the champagne was spelled so that paranormals would feel heightened effects of the alcohol. It was a trick used for supernaturals, who often had to drink twice as much just to feel a little tipsy. Which meant that if Felicia, who happened to be a witch, drank too much, she'd be not only throwing herself at Christoph later, but also everyone else around her. Spelled alcohol made her lose every last bit of her inhibitions.

She put the flute down in one of the holders and reached for a crab puff. After she'd finished off three, one of the bridesmaids shoved a dildo bouquet into her hands and said, "Time to see some delicious man-flesh."

The bus had stopped in front of Witchin' Impossible, and the vampires were already climbing out. Felicia glanced around through blurry eyes and blinked. When she stood, the world spun.

"Oh crap," she said, holding on to the pole in the middle of the bus.

"Are you okay?" a sweet brunette asked, placing a hand on the small of her back.

Felicia shook her head. "No. I think I drank too much."

The brunette frowned. "You only had one glass."

Had she? Felicia couldn't quite recall in that moment.

"Did you eat anything today?"

"Sure. Some of the crab puffs."

The brunette grimaced. "Oh no. Didn't anyone tell you those were spelled, too?"

"No." But she should've known, shouldn't she? The Cristal was spelled. What had made her think the food wouldn't be?

"Come on. I'll get you some coffee and some bread or something."

In a haze, Felicia stumbled out of the bus after the vampire. The world was a pretty array of sparkling light and color. And before she knew it, she could feel music strumming in her bones.

"Sit here," her new friend ordered.

Felicia plopped down on a velvet chair, running her hand over the soft seat. "I love this place. The chairs make me think of the old castle on the hill. When we were kids, we used to go up there and visit Madame Cherie. Her place was decorated like a French castle. Velvet and silk everywhere."

"What is she going on about?" someone asked.

"Never mind. She's just a little high. Too much fun food. Waiter? Can I order a pot of coffee and something untainted? Got any protein back there?"

"Wings," a man said with laughter in his tone. "Someone started bingeing a little early did they?" He crouched down in front of Felicia and tilted her head up so he could look her in the eye. "Getting wild tonight, eh, Fe?"

"Cooper?" She placed a hand on his cheek. "This is their fault. I think I need water."

"You got it, party girl." Her friend patted her hand and disappeared. Felicia sat in a dazed, blissed-out haze as the women around her started hooting and hollering. She didn't know how much time had passed before Cooper reappeared. "Here. Drink this. It should help."

Felicia gulped down the mint flavored water. Almost immediately her vision started to clear.

"Eat the chicken, too." Cooper slid a cardboard bowl full of chicken strips in front of her.

"Where did these come from?" she asked just before she took a bite.

"Next door."

"The healer, Mystia?" Felicia asked, her eyebrows raised.

"Yep. She says you owe her one." Cooper pushed back his surfer-boy blond hair and grinned at her.

"I don't know what it is you have over that girl, but the last time I asked her for help she huffed out a couple of swear words and slammed the door in my face." She took another bite of the chicken and started to feel like herself again.

Cooper gave her a half smile and shrugged as he glanced away, suddenly looking slightly awkward.

Felicia narrowed her eyes and peered at him. "It's too dark to tell, but I'd swear you're blushing. Are you dating Mystia?"

"I... I'm not sure," he said and then laughed. "I'd say yes, but she'd say no. So..."

"You are dating her." Felicia sat up and smacked him on his shoulder, her eyes wide. "That prim little witch is dating a stripper!"

"Dancer," Cooper corrected.

"Whatever. You strip down to your banana hammock four nights a week while brides throw money at you. I'd call that a stripper."

"It pays the bills," he said, completely unembarrassed.

Felicia laughed. "I know and I couldn't care less. But Mystia? Man, that's funny. You know how many times I've seen her turn her nose up at brides who ask for her miracle hangover cure? Her self-righteousness is off the charts."

He frowned, and his expression turned stormy. "She's not like that, Fe. I wish you'd give her a break. She saved your ass tonight, didn't she?"

Felicia glanced at the water and the chicken and suddenly felt bad. "You're right. She did. But I'm still not clear on why?" She eyed Cooper and gave him a teasing smile. "Are you just that good in bed?"

"Yes." He snickered. "But that's not why," he said after his mirth died down. "I told her what happened, and she felt bad for you. Said she can't stand it when people are spelled against their will. She said as long as you stay away from alcohol the rest of the night, her antidote should remain effective."

"Thank the gods. I have a date later." She grinned at

Cooper, but before he could respond, the crowd noise shifted from a dull roar to a loud chorus of disapproval. One of the women screamed, and another shouted for someone to stop.

Both Felicia and Cooper jumped up and started running toward the stage. Felicia had no idea what could be happening, but whoever was involved, she was sure to know them. The island wasn't that big. And she was on a first name basis with every one of the dancers. If one of them was hurt—Felicia gasped as the stage came into view.

"Bradley, no!" she cried, pressing her hand to her throat in horror. Her eyes were bulging as she watched her friend drink viciously from Bianca's neck. The bride was limp in his arms, and if Felicia hadn't known she was a vampire herself, she'd have been certain Bianca was dead.

Cooper jumped over the women in the crowd, most of them frozen in horror. Two had gotten onto the stage. One was pulling Bradley's hair, while the other was sitting on the floor, her miniskirt bunched up around her waist, revealing her lime green G-string as she tried to rip Bianca away from his vice-like grip. Neither appeared to be having any affect, and the entire scene resembled a bad reenactment of a Monty Python episode.

"Out of the way!" Cooper yelled to the two women as he grabbed Bradley's neck and squeezed. His fingers dug into the vampire's throat, cutting off his ability to feed. It was a self-defense move all paranormals were taught in grade school to ward off rogue vampires. But vampire attacks were so rare these days, Felicia was surprised she even remembered it.

Bradley dropped Bianca and turned on Cooper, his eyes wild as if he were feral. What in the hell had happened to him? Bradley was the fun-loving guy who spent his days off night skiing all over the world. If he'd been human, he'd likely have been a ski bum, the happy-go-lucky guy who was everyone's friend.

Felicia ran up the stairs at the side of the stage and rushed to Bianca's side. The vampire had two puncture wounds on her throat, and her skin had turned snow white. Goddess above, how much blood had he taken?

"I need a plasma pouch, now!" Felicia yelled. But the crowd was too loud, and no one appeared to hear her. "Son of a witch." Felicia stood and summoned all of her will. She didn't use her magic often. Ever since her cousin Esmerelda had cast that evil curse, magic really took the devil out of her. But Felicia didn't have a choice now. She needed to get Bianca out of there before the vampire went into a deep sleep and didn't wake up. If too much blood was lost, a vampire could sleep for decades.

With magic pulsing in her veins, Felicia concentrated on Bianca and called, "There's a storm to weather, receive my will, let me be the one to carry you light as a feather."

Pure white light streamed from Felicia's fingertips. Her head swam and the world spun, but she took a deep breath and steadied herself. Then she focused on the vampire who was all lit-up with her magic, reached down, and picked her up. Without the spell, there was no way the five-foot-two, one hundred and ten-pound witch would've been able to carry the dead weight of the six-foot-tall vampire bride. But there she was, hauling Bianca through the riled up crowd.

"Holy hell," Dixie said from behind the bar when Felicia propped Bianca on one of the high-back bar stools. "She looks like death."

"Plasma pack. Now!" Felicia reached behind the bar and grabbed a towel. She immediately started to clean the bride's neck, but it was no use. Blood had spilled on her flirty party dress, and no matter what Felicia did to try to clean her up, until she had a change of clothes she'd look like a vampire-slayer victim... on the night before her wedding. Poor thing.

"Here." Dixie, the pixie witch who owned the bar, shoved the warmed pouch into Felicia's hands and then stabbed the bag with a straw.

Felicia positioned the straw into Bianca's mouth and squeezed, praying the taste of the plasma would automatically cause her feeding instinct to kick in.

Blood ran down Bianca's chin, but she didn't respond.

"Dammit, Bianca, come on!" Felicia shook the vampire, hoping it would wake her.

"Neutralize your spell," Dixie said. "She likely can't control her responses with all that magic crawling all over her."

"Right." Felicia snapped her fingers and her magic vanished.

Bianca immediately fell to the left and would've landed on the sticky floor if it hadn't been for the man who appeared out of nowhere and grabbed her.

"Thank you—" Felicia glanced up into familiar steel-blue eyes. "What are you doing here?"

Christoph gave her a tight smile. "The groom was summoned."

CHAPTER 3

"Summoned? By who?" Felicia squeezed the plasma bag again and sighed in relief when she saw Bianca's throat working.

"Some stupid bachelor party treasure hunt thing. It's not important." He wrapped an arm around Bianca as the bride vampire leaned into him, her hands now clutching the pouch as she sucked down the last of the plasma.

Felicia glanced at Dixie. "Can you get another one ready?"

"On it," the bartender said and disappeared into the back.

"What happened here?" Christoph's chilly tone sent a shiver up Felicia's spine as he finally took in Bianca's disheveled state.

She met his angry, accusatory eyes and actually took a step back, raising her hands in a stop motion.

"Whoa, there, Mr. Protective Pants. Don't turn your ire on me. I'm the one who made sure she got out of the line of fire and got plasma pumped back into her."

He glanced at the chaos still going on around them and scowled deeper. "How did this happen? Didn't you help her set up this night with the vamps from down under thing?"

Dammit. She had recommended Witchin' Impossible to Bianca when the bride had ordered dildo bouquets. But there'd never been a vampire attack before. This wasn't her fault. "Almost every bride has her bachelorette party here. In ten years, there's never been any sort of problem. And certainly never any attacks. This"—Felicia waved a hand at the chaos—"is *not* normal."

He raised one judgmental eyebrow. "Then why is everyone standing around like it is? Doesn't this place have security?"

"No," Dixie said from behind the bar. "Our vampires *are* the security. They are supposed to keep an eye on the staff and the customers. Why would we need to hire security when we have the most powerful paranormals working here on a nightly basis?"

"Then where are they?" he asked with a growl.

Felicia scanned the chaos and realized that he was right. In her rush to help Bianca, she hadn't realized the only vampire who had stepped up to take on Bradley was Cooper. Where *were* the other vamps? She didn't have time to find out, however, because at just that moment Bianca snapped out of her haze, clamped her hand over her wound, and jumped off the stool.

"Who did this to me?" she demanded, looking between Felicia and Christoph.

Christoph waved a hand at Felicia. "Ask your new bestie."

Bianca scrunched up her face in confusion at him. "Isn't she your date?"

"Not anymore," he said, grabbing her hand. "Come on. Let's get you out of here before trouble finds you again."

Not anymore? Was he seriously blaming this fiasco on her? She was tempted to give him a piece of her mind, but decided he wasn't worth making a scene. She didn't need to fool around with a jackass.

He started to pull Bianca toward the exit, but she dug in her heels. "What do you think you're doing?"

"Bianca," he said impatiently.

"Don't Bianca me. Didn't she just save me from going into an extended sleep? Isn't she the only one who was looking out for me before you got here?" She turned and stared at the crowd watching Cooper and Bradley fight as if they were in a cage match. All the patrons were crowded around them, cheering and jeering as if they'd been tranced into a frenzy. "Look at them, Christoph. They've lost their minds. All six of my bridesmaids are out there waving their dildos in the air, screaming for one vamp to rip the other's head off. I mean, if I didn't know better, I'd think they were advocating for a castration."

Christoph's face pinched as he lowered his hands and covered his crotch.

Felicia couldn't help it. She burst out laughing.

He withered another glare in her direction, but she only laughed harder. Bianca glanced between them and clamped her hand over her mouth as she started to chuckle.

"You have to admit, Chris, you do look fairly ridiculous," she said, patting his arm.

He glanced down at his linked hands and quickly pulled them apart. "Just don't say another word about castration, all right?"

"Fine," she snorted. "But we can't leave until we round up all my girls. If this fight continues, who knows what could happen to them. Besides," she narrowed her eyes as she stared at the two vampires still fighting, "I owe that blond vampire a piece of fang."

Felicia didn't like the sound of that. One vampire fight was quite enough for one evening. "Listen, if I can get the girls over here, will you just go back to the party bus? Bradley isn't going anywhere. There's plenty of time for him to make some sort of retribution for his attack. But the most important thing is that you're getting married tomorrow. Wouldn't your time be better spent at the healer where you can get this documented and have a better legal case?"

"Legal case?" Christoph asked. "You think this is going to be settled by a payoff?"

"Um..." Felicia didn't know how to answer that. She could be honest and answer yes. It would be the most civilized way. Bradley would be forced to pay a hefty sum, and it would go on his record. One or two more attacks and that would be the end of him. Her stomach turned as she thought about what could happen to him if he made one more false move.

"Yes," Bianca answered in her place. "I'll need the documentation anyway, otherwise Jasper will think the worst."

"No he won't," Christoph said stubbornly, crossing his arms over his chest. "My brother—"

"Is the most jealous vampire on the planet. If he's not convinced I didn't just *let* that vampire dancer bite me, there won't be a wedding. Mark my words," Bianca said, tears filling her eyes.

"Oh, no. It's okay," Felicia said, putting her arm around Bianca and tugging her in for a sideways hug. "We'll work this out. Let me get the girls' attention."

"How—" Bianca started.

Driven to do whatever she could to help the wedding go off without a hitch, Felicia called up her magic one more time. The brilliant white light coated her fingers as she said, "Keepers of the love bouquets, return to me."

Six identical dildo bouquets shot straight up in the air and started to spin. A hush fell over the crowd as everyone stopped egging on the two vampires still fighting on the stage, and tilted their heads up to watch the possessed foliage. Amused that she'd caught everyone's attention so easily, Felicia waved her hand back and forth, making the bouquets sway in the air.

Then she pointed a finger and made a circle. The bouquets stopped spinning and slowly started to move in the opposite direction as they continued to dance high above everyone.

The dildos bobbed up and down, and Felicia couldn't help the giggle that escaped from her lips. When she moved to cover her mouth, the bouquets suddenly whipped in her direction, flying over the heads of the transfixed crowd. Felicia threw her hands up and caught the first and second ones. A third one went right past her head, bounced off a light fixture, and fell to the floor. Bianca grabbed two of them, but the last one was headed straight for Christoph. Mortified, Felicia reached up to grab it but bumped it instead, and the bouquet upended itself and fell dildo-first, right into Christoph's lap.

He tried to jump off the stool as he reached for it, but just as his hand wrapped around the base of the bouquet two things happened; the loud buzz of the vibrator filled Felicia's ears, and he tripped over the base of the stool, sending him stumbling in Felicia's direction. She tried to move out of his way to keep from getting trampled, but instead ended up right in his path. He stumbled into her, and in the process, the tip of the vibrating dildo ended up right in her crotch.

The tingling sensation rippled through her and she let out a shocked gasp, trying to move away. Only it was no use as she was pinned between him and the bar... with the Jack Rabbit hitting its exact target. Despite her mortification, her entire body heated with pleasure. With his long lean body pressed against her and the vibrating tip hitting its mark, she had to squeeze her eyes shut to keep from squirming. She dug her nails into his arms and bit her lower lip before forcing out, "This is moving a little fast considering we haven't even had our first date, isn't it? Besides, I'd prefer to explore the real thing before we move on to toys."

"What?" he asked, staring down at her lips.

"Um," she pushed gently at his solid form. When he didn't budge, she tapped the arm still holding the vibrator bouquet. "Could you please remove your hand. The, uh, bouquet is invading my personal space."

He took a step back, taking the pleasure stick with him, and stared at the bouquet for just a moment before his cheeks took on a pink hue.

Felicia wondered briefly if she'd ever seen a vampire blush before. And did that mean he'd fed recently? Probably.

"I'm... oh Christ. Sorry." He tossed the bouquet on the bar where it rumbled against the polished wood.

"Oh my god!" Bianca said and howled with laughter. "I knew these bouquets were going to be fun, but I had no idea just how *much* fun they'd be."

All of her bridesmaids were circled around her, each of them giggling like school girls as they watched the awkward exchange between Felicia and Christoph.

"Honey," Bianca said, placing her hand on his arm. "If you don't take that girl to bed tonight, someone else will."

"Excuse me," Felicia and Christoph said at the same time.

Bianca just patted his arm. "See that look on her face? Take note. It's the one that says she's ready when you are." The blond vampire winked at Felicia, then snapped her fingers and said, "Come on girls. It's time to get out of this joint. I've had about all the fun I can take for one night."

As Bianca led the pack of women toward the front door, Christoph stared down at Felicia. "I'm sorry. I don't know what just happened there."

"Forget it." Felicia glanced away, unable to look him in the eye. She was more than mortified. Bianca was right. She was ready for this man. Hot to trot, her grandmother would've said. The only problem was he'd been a jackass, accusing her of being to blame for Bianca's attack. And just because the man, who admittedly had a way with a vibrator, was too sexy for his own good, didn't mean she was going to throw herself at someone who was a jerk.

"Felicia," he said, his tone softer now. Reaching up, he brushed a lock of her long dark hair out of her eyes. "I apologize. What I said… it was uncalled for. Thank you for helping her."

"Sure. I would've done it for anyone."

With his gaze locked on hers, he nodded. "I believe you would."

Neither of them said anything for a moment. Then he closed his eyes and took another step back. "Rain check on the breakfast date?"

Disappointment made her gut tighten, but she was careful to keep a neutral expression as she said, "Rain check."

"Tomorrow night after the wedding?" he asked.

Everything inside Felicia longed to say yes, but instead she shook her head and made up an excuse. "I can't. We have another wedding I have to prep florals for. Maybe the next time you're in town," she added, knowing he wouldn't be coming back anytime soon. Vampires rarely got married. When you're immortal, forever is a very long time.

"Right." He ran a hand through his hair, sexual frustration rolling off him as he gazed at her hungrily.

She didn't know why, but his reaction made her angry. In that moment, his motivation for asking her out was far too blatant. Yeah, she'd said yes to a date, fully expecting to have a hot fling with him. But she'd liked him, too. He'd made her laugh, and she'd thought he liked her. But the way he'd reacted toward her after Bianca's attack and his quick shift to wanting to get her into bed just rankled.

"See you around," she said as she took a step forward to move past him. An intense shiver of desire seized her as her bare arm brushed against his. She could have sworn she heard him suck in a sharp breath. Satisfaction washed over her. Vampires didn't need to breathe, but they often did when they experienced intense emotions like anger, frustration, and in this case, desire.

With a force of sheer will, she didn't look back as

she made her way toward the exit. Instead she focused on the stage where Cooper and Bradley had finally stopped fighting. Bradley was kneeling off to the side, shaking his head as he stared at Witchin' Impossible's club manager in disbelief. Blood stained his chin and chest. Then he stood and shook his head more forcefully. She couldn't hear his words over the music and chatter of the club, but the confusion and disbelief in his expression made her frown. What was going on up there? Did he not remember what happened?

Cooper was sitting on one of the prop chairs, savage fang marks covering his neck. Not the neat pinholes left after a feeding, but the ones left by an enraged vampire intent on ripping another's head off. She started to make her way toward the stage, but stopped dead in her tracks as a blood-curdling scream filled her ears.

Felicia spun and had a direct view of Bianca standing in the open front door, her hands fisted as she vibrated with pure anger.

CHAPTER 4

*C*hristoph fixated his attention on Felicia's backside as she sauntered away from him. Clearly the witch had added an extra sway to her hips just to torture him. He could hardly blame her. Hadn't he basically accused her of being responsible for Bianca's attack?

He was an idiot. How could it be Felicia's fault that some vampire had helped himself to Bianca's blood? Bianca was trouble in stilettos and always had been. Or at least she had been right up until she'd gotten engaged to his brother Jasper last year. Since then she'd been a different vampire. Oh, she'd still been just as outrageous as always. The vibrator bouquets proved that well enough. But she had stopped crossing lines with random vampires and kept her flirting strictly in friend mode instead of pushing their buttons just to see how far she could take things before they got out of hand.

It wouldn't be a surprise to find out she'd slipped back into old habits the night before she was scheduled to promise herself to one man for the rest of her undead days. He'd cursed himself the moment he'd seen the indignation flash over Felicia's face. And that had been the moment he'd lost her. No date. No steamy weekend with the hot witch who'd already gotten under his skin.

He shook his head. It was just as well, he supposed. He already knew he liked her fire and spunk way too much. Even before taking her to bed, he was certain he wouldn't want to walk away come Monday afternoon. And relationships never had been his strong suit. Better to walk away before they even got started, he told himself.

With his eyes still glued to Felicia, he started to follow Bianca. But then just as he registered Bianca's scream, he watched Felicia spin and stare at the door, her expression scrunched up in confusion.

Christoph didn't hesitate. He sprang forward, ready to rip off the head of whoever was making that inhuman sound come from Bianca's throat. In less than a second, he was standing next to Bianca, speechless at the scene in front of him.

"Jasper, what the fuck are you doing?" He strode forward and yanked his brother off the neck of a tall brunette.

His brother snarled, blood staining his lips and his eyes wild.

"You fucking bastard!" Bianca forced out through a sob.

"Are you out of your mind?" Christoph asked. "You're getting married tomorrow."

"Was getting married tomorrow," Bianca said.

The wild look in his brother's eyes vanished, and Jasper first focused on Christoph. He straightened and stepped back, shaking off Christoph's grip. "What are you doing, man?"

Christoph ground his teeth together. "Trying to save your ass, but it looks like I'm too late." He glanced over his shoulder at Bianca and winced. Nothing was going to help his brother now.

"I can't believe you'd do this to me." She glanced at the brunette and wrinkled her nose. "What is she wearing? Are those... mom jeans and a crop top? And, oh my god, she's wearing *macramé* sandals." She visibly shuddered. "Jasper, have you no standards?"

Christoph turned his attention to the dazed woman standing beside Jasper. She had mascara smudged under her bright blue eyes, her hair looked like something out of a bad eighties movie, and there was a small butterfly tattoo on the top of her foot. She definitely looked like she'd stepped out of a time machine.

"Lemon?" Felicia brushed past them both to rush up to the other woman. She wrapped an arm around her shoulders and asked, "Are you all right?"

"Huh?" The woman blinked rapidly as if she was trying to focus.

"You're okay now," Felicia soothed, her features soft and inviting. Something inside Christoph shifted, and he found himself wanting to move to her side just to be near all her warmth. The realization shook him, and he took a step back, needing to put even more distance between them. What the hell was wrong with him? He barely even knew the woman and here he was acting like a love-sick teenager. "Want me to call your sister Hildie? Have her come get you?" she asked the woman.

"Hildie is gone," Lemon said, shaking her head. She pressed a hand to her neck and frowned. She glanced around at Bianca, Christoph, and Jasper, and then once again focused on Felicia. "What happened?"

"You tangled with a groom vampire… again," Felicia said, disapproval in her tone, recalling two summers ago when Lemon tried to bag the richest vampire on the east coast. She'd broken into his hotel room and waited for him on his bed… naked. The vampire had been all too willing, and when his fiancée walked in on them in the act, all hell had broken loose. The incident had been in the gossip rags for months and brought the whole island unwanted attention. No one wanted infidelity associated with the island—weddings drove the city's entire economy. Romance and happily-ever-afters were the bread and butter of Witch Island. Lemon's stunt only earned her the scorn of the town. It was around then when she'd turned into a recluse and started acting strange.

"I did?" Her brow crinkled as she concentrated. It took her moment, but her gaze finally landed on Jasper. A tiny, self-satisfied smile claimed her lips. "Right. I remember now." She raised a delicate hand and wiggled her fingers at him.

Bianca growled. Christoph coughed to hide his chuckle. He knew Bianca hadn't changed that much. As nice as it was to see her settle down with his brother, he had missed her angst and had even worried she'd turned herself into something she wasn't just to please Jasper. He turned and glared at his brother. While he appreciated seeing Bianca's fire, he sure as hell didn't care for his brother hurting her by feeding off of some vampire groupie.

Jasper backed up, an air of fear surrounding him as he glanced at his bride. "Bianca, I—"

"Just don't, Jas. I don't want to hear it. I told you not to ask me to marry you if you weren't done fanging around. You should've listened the first time."

"But I—"

She held her hand up, glaring at him. "There's nothing to say. We're done." Bianca glanced at Felicia. "I forfeit my deposit. The wedding's off. If there's a bill to pay, send it to Jasper."

"Bianca!" Jasper rushed after his former bride as she strode off, her head held high. When he caught up with her, she spun on him, her eyes blazing with pure hatred.

"Get away from me," she said through clenched teeth. "We're through." Bianca took off running. Jasper stood there for a moment, gripping the back of his neck with one hand as he stared at the ground. Then he straightened, and a look of determination settled on his handsome face. Without a word, he took off through the parking lot after his bride.

"This isn't going to end well," Christoph said.

"Of course it isn't," Felicia said with a scowl. "He cheated."

He gazed at her, curious about her righteous indignation. "You seem pretty upset for someone who just met them a few days ago."

Felicia turned narrowed eyes on him then raised one eyebrow. "Is there a reason why you aren't? Your best friend and your brother? Is it possible you didn't *want* them to be together? Are you jealous?"

"What?" he said, that familiar pit forming in his stomach again. Was she just like all the others? Convinced that a man couldn't be friends with a woman without some hidden attraction going on? Every woman he'd ever dated had been the same; certain he wanted his best friend instead of them. Suddenly tired, he shook his head. "Jealous? Of Jasper? No. Not even close."

She pursed her lips as she studied him, her expression curious. "Then why do you seem like you don't care about what just happened?"

He shrugged. "I don't know. Maybe because Bianca has a flair for drama? Because I've witnessed more breakups and makeups than I can count, and it's likely this union will be back on just as soon as Jasper figures out how to explain this one." He waved a hand at Lemon, who was sitting on a bench vaping.

Felicia shook her head. "She's not going to forgive him. Not after that breach of trust. At least not any time soon. Did you see the look on her face? She was devastated."

"She'll forgive him," Christoph said, nodding with confidence. "Eventually."

Felicia gave him a pained look. "I don't have time to wait for eventually. Do you have any idea how much it costs to have orchids flown in on this island? My margins were already razor thin on this job. If Bianca and your brother don't go through with this wedding, I'm going to be eating rice and beans for the rest of the month."

He shook his head. "Don't worry about that. Jasper will pay whatever your fee is even if Bianca doesn't come to her senses."

"I hope you're right."

Heavy footsteps pounded on the pavement and Jasper reappeared, his expression furious. "Where is that witch?"

"Which witch?" Christoph asked, glancing at Felicia.

She held up her hands in a *whoa* motion. "I didn't do anything other than eat too many crab puffs."

"The one who put a spell on me. The nineties throwback with the blue eyeshadow."

"Lemon?" Felicia said, waving toward the bench.

Christoph glanced over to where the witch had been sitting just a few moments before, only to find the bench empty. He frowned. She couldn't have left without them noticing. She'd have had to walk right past them.

"Where did she go?" Felicia asked him. "Did you see her leave?"

He shook his head, scanning the night. The moon shone down on the courtyard, illuminating the blooming jasmine that covered an eight-foot-tall rock wall. He cleared his throat. "She couldn't have just vanished into thin air, could she?"

"Actually..." Felicia tapped a finger on her chin. "Lemon has some unusual powers. It might be possible."

"Where can I find her?" Jasper asked, his expression sinister.

"I don't—" Felicia shook her head. "Maybe you should cool off a bit before you go see her."

"Cool off! That witch spelled me somehow, and now my fiancée has called off the wedding and is threatening to flee not just the island, but the country, too. If she does that, it'll take me years to find her. You have no idea how stubborn Bianca can be. It's imperative that I fix this tonight."

Christoph snorted. "You're right. You won't find her."

"And neither will you, brother," Jasper said, glaring at him. "Do you think for a moment she's going to get in touch with you if she thinks you'll tell me where she is?"

He sobered and shook his head. Gods. Jasper was

right. Once Bianca had gotten so mad at him, she'd disappeared for five years. He'd had a hunch she was in New Orleans, had even looked for her there a handful of times, but somehow she'd always known when he rolled into town and made herself scarce. It wasn't until one spring day when he was roaming Amsterdam that she'd just shown up and acted as if nothing had ever happened. Six months later, she finally invited him to her penthouse condo in the middle of the French Quarter. He smiled thinking about their time on Bourbon Street.

"Christoph, for fuck's sake, none of this is funny. Do you want to lose your best friend again?" Jasper asked.

"No and no," he said, shaking his head. "You find Lemon. I'll go talk to Bianca."

"You can't talk to her," he said. "She's off at that exclusive spa on the other side of the island. She's already said she'll leave word to keep us both out." Jasper turned to Felicia once more. "Please, I need to find that witch. Where does she live?"

Felicia sighed. "I can't tell you that."

Jasper moved so fast, his body became a blur. He stopped right in front of her, standing so close his body was brushing up against hers. "I don't think you seem to understand what's happening right now. Either you tell me where she is, or I'll sue you and your little shop into oblivion."

"Sue me? For what?" she asked indignantly.

"Jas—" Christoph started.

"For feeding her plasma without her consent. She's a vegetarian."

"Are you kidding me?" Felicia asked, her eyes flashing with outrage. "She lost too much blood. Synthetics weren't going to save her."

"You don't know that," he said, his voice hard and cold as ice. "There is a reason Bianca doesn't drink blood. It makes her... aggressive and rash. And see what she did after you force-fed her? She fled and called off the wedding."

"Jasper!" Christoph moved to stand in front of his brother, his muscles bunched in irritation. What the fuck was his brother up to? He could be a bastard when he had his hackles up, but he'd never seen him threaten someone who didn't completely deserve it before. "You know she's only pissed because she saw you cheating on her again. You can't pin this on Felicia."

"That will be for the judge to decide." He glanced over Christoph's shoulder and glared at Felicia. "What do you say, witch? Are you going to help me or risk losing that pretty little floral shop of yours?"

CHAPTER 5

Rage boiled in Felicia's blood as she stared at Jasper. The vampire, whom she'd previously believed was entirely too handsome for his own good, now had an ugly twist to his lips, and his eyes were void of any emotion other than cold determination. She wanted to scream or lash out. She didn't need this crap in her life. Why was this suddenly her problem? All she'd been trying to do was help Bianca, and this is how she got repaid? She was half-tempted to conjure a cactus chair and shove him into it. That'd show him when he had cacti needles up his ass.

"I was going to say I can't tell you where she lives because I don't know." She crossed her arms over her chest and tried her best to keep her magic in check. If she got too angry, the next thing she knew he actually would be sitting on a cactus. "Lemon is extremely private. And while I know she has a place somewhere here on the island, she moves so often, no one can keep up."

"Someone has to know," he snarled.

"Only her landlord."

"And her neighbors," Christoph added. "Right?"

She shook her head. "No. Not if she put a cloaking spell over her place. They'd never see her coming or going."

"I guess you have your work cut out for you then," Jasper said. "Find her before tomorrow at noon, or I'll be filing that lawsuit."

"You can't do that!" she yelled as he strode away, but she knew he could. And he'd likely win too. He had way too much money, while she had just a meager savings. He'd bury her in court costs alone.

"Watch me," the vampire said just before he disappeared into the parking lot.

"Jackass," Christoph muttered under his breath.

"I was going to go with assface buttboil, but I guess jackass works." Felicia pushed back her hair and racked her brain, trying to determine a starting point for finding Lemon.

Christoph grinned. "Assface buttboil?"

Goddess, he's beautiful, she thought. Then she sighed. She suddenly had more problems than just a stupid curse that guaranteed her a lifetime of singlehood. "I think it has a certain ring to it."

"I'm going to get that monogramed on his guest towels."

"His guest towels? Surely you can come up with something much more diabolical than that."

"Sure. But the beauty of this plan is that Jasper is extremely self-centered. He also cares entirely too much what other people think of him. He won't ever notice a new monogram on his guest towels. It's guaranteed to embarrass the shit out of him, and anyone who knows him well enough to stay at his place will know he had nothing to do with the change."

Felicia stared at him in disbelief. "That is... completely pedestrian, Christoph. I'm almost embarrassed for you."

He studied her for a moment then threw his head back and laughed. "I'm really going to enjoy hanging out with you this weekend. How about you help me figure out ways to torture his ass?"

"As fun as that sounds," she said, unable to help the smile that tugged at her lips, "I think I'm going to be too busy looking for Lemon. Maybe look me up next time a buddy is getting married."

She turned, intending to head for the path that ran along the seashore toward her floral shop, but just after she rounded the building and slipped through a wrought iron gate, Christoph appeared in front of her, blocking her path.

"Wait just a second," he said. "Don't you want some help?"

She tilted her head back and gazed up into his troubled, steel-blue eyes. "If you really want to help me, Christoph, you'll talk your brother into dropping the threat of a lawsuit. This isn't in any way my fault. He's the one who was fanging Lemon."

His brows pinched together as a pained look flashed over his face. "You're right. None of this is your fault. But I can't talk him out of the threat. Not tonight anyway."

She let out an irritated breath and moved to push past him. "Then you're useless to me."

"I can help you find this witch, can't I?" he said stubbornly.

"I don't know how," she said with a defeated sigh. "Can you scent her out or something?"

"No. Not unless she's bleeding." He gave her a wry smile. "But let's try to avoid that."

She shook her head. "Listen, thanks for the offer, but I think it's better if I do this alone."

"Why?" he called after her as she rushed down the trail.

Because, she thought, *you're too effing distracting*. That playful, devilish grin, his soulful, steel-blue eyes, and those lips. Dammit. She wanted them on her, and at that moment, she didn't have time to dick around. "I need to concentrate," she said truthfully and quickened her pace.

With each step, Felicia kept an ear trained to the trail behind her. Had he followed her? It didn't sound like it, but vampires could easily move in super-stealth mode. More importantly, did she want him to follow her? An emphatic *yes* sounded in her mind. And instead of graciously accepting his help, she'd blown him off, just like she did with every other attractive man who ever walked into her life. Dammit. Why couldn't anything ever go right for even one night?

"Effing, Esmerelda!" she cried into the night, hating her cousin more than ever. It was time to admit to herself that Esmerelda's damned spell had been more effective than she'd been willing to believe. All these years, she'd used the excuse that her relationships couldn't last anyway, so why bother. But the last few times she'd talked herself into even a short-term fling, disaster had followed, making it clear she was doomed to be alone forever.

She froze on the path, her heart hammering against her ribcage. Holy hell. The trouble brewing between Jasper and Bianca really was her fault. Deep in her gut, she knew that if she hadn't accepted Christoph's date none of the disastrous events of the night would've happened. She couldn't prove it, but everything inside her knew her suspicions were true.

Felicia was cursed, and now it was affecting other people.

Jasper was right. She was to blame.

Or, more specifically, Esmerelda was to blame.

Her cousin's deceptively sweet face swam in Felicia's mind. Then she started to run, desperate to escape the memory that was bound to bombard her. But as her footsteps pounded on the soft earth, Felicia's surroundings faded and she knew she'd once again be thrust back in time to the one place she couldn't bear to go.

Night faded to a warm sunny day. A light breeze flowed from the bluff and rustled Felicia's hair, blowing a long, curled strand into her eyes. She brushed it back and looked out at the churning sea. "Isn't it lovely, Esmerelda?"

Her cousin stood beside her, her lips twisted into a scowl. "What's so great about it? It's dark and angry and full of heartache."

Felicia turned her attention to Esmerelda, really seeing her for the first time that morning. The petite blonde had dark circles under her red-rimmed eyes, her hair was tied up into a messy bun, and there was a scratch down the left side of her cheek. "Oh my goddess, Esme, what happened?"

She let out a humorless laugh. "You just now noticed I look like hell?"

"I'm sorry. I was busy decorating the arch when you got here. You know how I get caught up in my work. Did something happen with Chad?"

"Did something happen with Chad?" she mimicked in a little girl's voice. "Like you don't know. You think that innocent act is going to work on me? I know you too well to believe that pile of bullshit."

The pure venom in Esmerelda's tone made Felicia take a step back as shock took over. She'd never heard her cousin speak to anyone the way she was speaking to her, her best friend and the person she'd grown up with. "Esme, what are you talking about?"

"What am I talking about?" she yelled, her voice echoing across the clearing. "How about the fact that you stole my fiancé? That he called off the wedding and told me he's in love with you?"

Felicia was utterly speechless as she stared at her cousin, unable to comprehend what she'd just said. Chad was in love with her? She shook her head, clearly not understanding. "Chad and I aren't—"

"Don't even try to deny it, Fe. I've seen the way the two of you are together. What happened? You saw us happy together and finally figured out he's the love of your life? Couldn't stand to see us happy? I can't believe you'd do this to me. I thought you loved me like a sister. But no, you're the worst kind of person out there. You pretend to be so good, so loving, so perfect. But you're not. You're just a back-stabbing witch who thinks nothing of taking whatever you want for yourself with no regard for other people."

Completely stunned, Felicia just stood there, her mouth open, blinking at Esmerelda. Finally, she said, "This is a cruel joke, right? Chad and I—"

"I don't want to hear it!" Esme screamed and flew at Felicia, knocking her to the earth.

Felicia landed hard on her backside, and anger finally broke through her shock. "Don't put your hands on me. I know you're upset, but—"

A fist came out of nowhere and connected with Felicia's eye with impressive force.

"Oomph." *Oh hell no*, Felicia thought as she clutched at her throbbing head. Her cousin was out of control. And Felicia was finding it far too difficult to find any sort of sympathy for her when she was being assaulted.

"I should've gut-punched you, then you'd know how I feel," Esmerelda whispered into Felicia ear.

Felicia lost all sense of control and reared up, grabbing her cousin around the waist and hauling her down to the earth with her. The pair punched, kicked, and scratched. Grass and mud flew as both witches grappled to subdue the other one. Finally, Felicia grabbed both of Esmerelda's wrists, and with a cry befitting a warrior princess, she rolled on top of her cousin, sat on her, and pinned her arms down.

"Listen," she said, breathing heavily. "I don't know why Chad thinks I'm the love of his life. Because he certainly—"

"Shut up!" Esmerelda roared as magic instantly coated her arms and rushed to her fingertips. "From earth to water and air to sea, from this day forward you'll be unlucky in love, I will it to be."

Magic shot from Esmerelda with a force so impressive, it threw Felicia backward a good ten feet, slamming her into one of the enchanted rose bushes. Upon impact, pain radiated over her bare arms and legs as the thick thorns tore into her skin. She let out a shriek of pain before her vision blurred and darkness took her.

She woke tangled in the rose bush. Everything hurt. Her head, her arms, her legs, her chest. The ache in her breastbone was from the force of the spell Esmerelda had thrown at her. But everything else was from the physical fight and the unfortunate landing in the rose bush. Felicia took a deep breath, trying to calm herself.

But the effort only brought a sharp stab of pain to her chest.

"Esmerelda, I need help," she forced out, hating that she had to ask the person who'd put her there to untangle her.

No answer.

"Dammit, Esmerelda. I know you're upset, but I'm hurt," she said through clenched teeth.

Still nothing.

Felicia tried in vain a few more times to get Esmerelda's attention, but her cousin was either ignoring her or had left. "That bitch," Felicia finally said, more upset by the abandonment than either the fight or the spell. She could understand her cousin taking out her pain and frustration on her, but to leave her there when she could be seriously hurt... it was unforgiveable.

Eventually, Felicia managed to crawl out of the bush, fresh scratches and all. And when she glanced around, she realized her fears were true. Her cousin had left. It was the last time she'd seen her.

It turned out that Chad had fallen in love with a man and had been too scared to tell anyone, so he'd lied to Esmerelda, telling her he had feelings for Felicia. Felicia had instantly forgiven him. He was her best friend, after all. And even though she didn't care for being used as an excuse, she understood he'd been terrified. Only Esmerelda hadn't shown back up on the island, and Felicia hadn't been able to find her. She'd figured her cousin would return after a few weeks, but she never did.

It wasn't until about six months later when Felicia realized Esmerelda's spell had taken root and doomed her to be unlucky in love for the rest of her life that she'd hired a private investigator. Even the PI she'd hired hadn't been able to find her. Every year Felicia tried again, and every year she was disappointed. Two years ago, she'd stopped, resigned to just live her life alone with her dog, Winston. She had Chad and Jonathon and the floral shop. What else did she need?

"Felicia, wake up," a deep voice resonated in her ear. "Come on, sweetheart. Open those gorgeous eyes and scowl at me some more."

She felt her brow crinkle as she tried to figure out who was talking to her.

He let out a low rumble of laughter. "That's it. Now show me the fire in your gaze."

Her eyelids flew open, and she blinked a couple of times, waiting for her vision to focus. And when it did, she stared right up into the steel-blue eyes of Christoph.

"Welcome back," he said with a gentle smile. "I was getting worried about you."

She pushed herself up and glanced around at the plush, stark-white room, noting she was lying on the most comfortable bed she'd ever encountered. "Where am I?"

"The Spellbound Hotel." That wicked grin claimed his lips again. "This is my room."

CHAPTER 6

*Christoph stared down at the lovely witch, brushing her tangled hair behind one ear. Thank the gods he'd taken off after her down that dark trail. One minute she was running at a steady pace, and the next she was lying flat out in the dirt.

He'd tried to wake her, but she'd been unresponsive other than the movement of her eyes behind her closed lids. He'd known then she was trapped in a memory. He'd witnessed another witch suffer the rare affliction years ago. There'd been nothing to do but wait it out. And there was no telling how long it'd take. Since he wasn't going to leave her out in the woods by herself in the middle of the night, he'd brought her back to his room.

He'd put her on her feet and held her up with one arm while he unlocked the door. Once he'd gained entry, he picked the witch back up and took her directly to the oversized shower stall. He'd found her in a puddle of mud, which was now caked in her hair and up and down the back of her clothes. She couldn't stay in them. Not unless he was willing to let his room become a mud pit.

He desperately wanted to strip her and put her under a spray of water, but that would have to wait. It was one thing to strip her down to her underclothes. It was entirely another to get her naked and manhandle her, no matter how good his intensions were. For now, all he needed to do was get her out of her dirty clothes and into a robe. If Bianca hadn't taken off, he'd ask her to handle it, but since she had, he didn't exactly have a choice.

First he undid her strappy sandals then moved on to her green fuzzy sweater. As he lifted the garment up her torso, he tried not to stare at her creamy white skin, or imagine what she would taste like as he explored every last inch of her. Damn, she was gorgeous. Flawless. And her curves were almost more than he could handle.

He glanced away. Devouring her with his eyes wasn't exactly noble. He pulled the sweater over her head, tossed it on the floor of the shower, and then lifted her up into a standing position. It didn't take long for him to divest her of her skirt. And if he was a better man, he'd have covered her up right then and there. But instead, his eyes zeroed in on the sunflower covering her mound. Her bra matched, with each breast sporting a cheerful sunflower right over her nipples.

He swallowed, suddenly salivating, dying to deflower her.

"Dammit." He cursed himself and placed her carefully back down onto the shower floor. He needed to get her covered up before he did something incredibly stupid. But mud caked her arms and legs, and he needed to clean her up first. Gritting his teeth against the need growing inside of him, he grabbed a wash cloth, ran a basin of hot water, and got to work.

∽

"Are you feeling okay? Do you need some caffeine or chocolate?" Christoph asked once Felicia finally returned to the land of the living. "I can call room service."

She gave him an odd look and cleared her throat. "How did you know about the caffeine and chocolate trick? Have you been stalking me or something?"

He laughed, completely entertained by her sass. "I promise you, if I'd been stalking you, I'd have made myself known long before this night." He got up and grabbed the cordless phone on the desk. "I had a... um, friend who would sometimes get trapped in her memories. Chocolate and caffeine always helped."

She pushed herself up into a sitting position. Her hair stuck out at all angles, making it look like she'd spent the night being ravaged in his bed. He bit back a groan as his insides tightened with the need that had been torturing him for the last hour.

"Can you get both? This one took it out of me," she said and grimaced when she reached up to do something with her hair. "Good goddess, I must look like something out of *Night of the Living Dead*."

"Interesting reference," he said dryly, holding back his mirth.

Her cheeks turned bright red just before she buried her face in both hands and muttered, "Sorry."

He laughed then ordered her a latte and a piece of the flourless chocolate cake. After he replaced the receiver, he turned back around to find her clutching her robe closed and glaring at him. "What? Wrong fit?"

"You stripped my clothes off?" she asked incredulously. "I don't even know you! You have some nerve. How am I supposed to know you didn't assault me while I was in my trance?" Glaring at him, she shoved her feet into the slippers at the side of the bed then stalked over to the door. "This is an extreme violation of my personal privacy."

"Whoa! Hold on there, Felicia. Give me two seconds to explain myself before you hang me up by my nads and stone me, will you?"

"Is that the preferred punishment for being a complete jackass? Because I could get behind that."

The urge to reflexively cover his junk was strong, but he forced himself to remain cool. "If you wish."

She appeared to think it over for a second as she tightened the robe around herself once again. When her brilliant blue eyes met his, she nodded once. "It is. Now you have about five seconds to convince me you aren't a creepy perv who felt me up while I was unconscious."

Creepy perv. Well, he'd been called worse, hadn't he? He cleared his throat. "I found you sprawled in a section of mud. If you check the back of your head, you'll likely still find some traces of it. I combed it out, but short of stripping you down to nothing and forcing you in the shower, I did the best I could."

She frowned and glanced back at the spotless white bedspread.

"I took you straight to the shower basin and cleaned you up in there." He walked over to the bathroom and opened the door. "See those?" He pointed inside at a pile of mud-stained towels. "That's only the last of them. Housekeeping already has the rest."

Her scowl turned to a grimace. "So you're saying you did shower me so you could clean me up?"

"No, I'm saying I set your mud-caked body in the shower while I got you out of your muddy clothes and into the robe. And I only did that because you were covered from head to toe in mud. If Bianca had been here, or any of her bridesmaids, I'd have asked them to do it, but since none of them were available, I did what I had to do. You wouldn't want to wake up with mud caked in your hair would you?"

"No," she said, still staring at the towels in the bathroom. After a moment, she pulled the robe away from her body and peeked at herself. A sigh of relief escaped her lips. "Thank the goddess I'm still wearing my underwear."

"We could remedy that," Christoph teased.

"Don't blow it, vamp-boy," she said, walking back over to him near the bed. "I was about to be grateful, but if you turn into a jackass again, I'll be spared the effort."

He held his hands up. "No jackass behavior here. I'm just your regular everyday Boy Scout, doing what he can to serve the pretty witch with a penchant for sunflowers."

She stared at him, her mouth open as if she was going to say something, but then she just smiled. "I do like my sunflowers. If you play your cards right, maybe you'll get a chance to see them again."

"Is that right?" he drawled, his eyes glinting at her.

"Well, not until I get to see you in all your glory first. It's only fair."

He mimed tipping his hat. "Whenever you're ready, I'm at your service."

She snorted. "I just bet you are." She started to move forward, but her knees seemed to give out and she ended up falling backward onto the bed. Her face was beyond pale, and her hands started to shake.

"Damn. Where is room service?" he muttered and walked over to the minibar. He opened it and cursed. The bar was stocked with champagne and synthetic blood. Clearly they'd customized it for a vampire.

"I'll be all right," she said, leaning against the headboard.

She sure as shit didn't look all right. And it was scaring the hell out of him. "I'll be right back."

"No!" she called out and reached out a hand. "Can you just stay? I don't want to plunge back into the memory."

He hesitated for half a second then nodded. "Of course."

Her head lolled to the side, but a second later, she jerked it back up.

He sat down next to her and opened his arms. "Need someone to lean on?"

Without a word, she wrapped her arms around his torso and pressed her head against his shoulder. He tightened his hold on her and breathed in her sweet cherry scent. How was that possible? Just an hour ago she'd been covered in mud, and even though he knew some was still lodged in her hair, he couldn't scent it at all. Nothing but sweet cherries. He let out a sigh, content for the first time in over a decade.

He stiffened when the realization hit him. The last time he'd been content with a woman in his arms, he'd fallen hard. He'd fallen twice before that, and in each case, he'd known the moment he'd held the woman in question.

He gritted his teeth. If she managed to feel anything for him, would he lose her too when she realized there was another woman in his life? One that was never going away?

"What's wrong?" she asked, gazing up at him through glassy eyes.

"Nothing, Felicia. Just wondering when the hell room service is going to show up so we can get you back in fighting shape."

Just then there was a knock on the door.

"Looks like they heard your summons," she said in a sleepy voice.

He gently disengaged from her embrace, and simultaneously felt relief and regret at the loss. He'd be happy to spend the rest of the weekend with her in his arms, but he knew if he did he'd regret it. Come Monday, he had a plane to catch. Whatever this was sparking between them, he couldn't let himself explore it. Not this time. He'd already vowed to not put himself in that position again.

Christoph pulled the door open and waved the man in. He took one look at Felicia and gave Christoph a knowing grin. Christoph gave him a flat stare.

The waiter cleared his throat. "Right then. Latte and flourless chocolate cake. Is there anything else we can get for you this evening, Mr. Parks?"

"No, thank you." He signed the ticket and before the waiter could even leave the room, Christoph had Felicia back in his arms again, holding the latte up for her to take a drink.

She gazed up at him with grateful eyes as she sipped the caffeine-filled drink. Instantly the spark returned to her eyes and her color improved.

"Welcome back," he said, smiling down at her.

"It's good to be back," she said and downed the rest

of the latte. When the cup was empty, she dug into the chocolate cake with gusto.

Christoph couldn't keep his eyes off her, the way her full lips wrapped around the fork and the pure pleasure that lit up her face. Everything inside of him wanted to taste her.

"Stop looking at me like that," she said.

"Like what?"

"Like you're the big bad wolf and I'm about to be your meal."

"My dessert," he corrected, his tone husky with need.

She froze, her fork filled with a piece of chocolate cake as she gazed up at him, her lips parted. Her breathing became just a little heavy, and her pupils dilated.

He knew the signs. She wanted him just as much as he wanted her. And if she hadn't just regained her strength after being trapped in a memory, or if they weren't supposed to be finding Lemon, he would've acted on her unspoken invitation. Hell, he almost acted on it anyway. Instead, he cleared his throat and stood. "When you're done, if you're up for it, I think it's time to start searching for the witch who spelled my brother."

CHAPTER 7

"Right," Felicia said, glancing back down at the chocolate cake. Had she really just been imagining licking it off his chest? She glanced back up at him and nodded to herself. Yes, yes she had.

Why did he have to be so perfect? And why did she have to be so damned attracted to him? His brother was literally making her life a nightmare. She couldn't have a fling with the brother of the man who was threatening to ruin her, could she?

He had taken care of her. Had already seen her in nothing but her sunflowers. What would be the harm?

Stop it, she told herself. *You already know the answer to that question.* With a heavy sigh, she shoved the rest of the cake in her mouth, swallowed, and then excused herself to the restroom. After rinsing her mouth out, she glanced in the mirror and realized she was still wearing the robe. Her clothes were nowhere to be found. Not that she wanted to put on her mud-caked outfit, but she couldn't exactly walk around town in a bathrobe.

"Um, Christoph?" she said as she strode out of the bathroom. "Where are my clothes?"

"I sent them out to be cleaned. I found some sweats and a T-shirt for you to wear for now."

Without a word, she took his clothes and disappeared into the bathroom again. When she reemerged, she had the waist band rolled down, the legs rolled up, and had tied the T-shirt into a knot at her waist. She wouldn't be winning any fashion awards, but at least she was decent.

"My shoes appear to be missing as well," she said.

He swept an approving gaze over her as he said, "They're getting cleaned, too."

"Okay, but I can't walk around barefoot."

"Nope. We can't have that." He winked, then swept her up into his arms and strode out of the room.

"Are you going to carry me around town while we look for Lemon?" she asked, her tone full of skepticism.

"I can if you wish," he said as he got on the elevator.

She clasped both hands behind his neck and giggled. "How about you take me to my place so I can check on Winston and get into some clothes that fit. Then we'll get to work. I have some ideas on where she might be tonight."

"Winston?" he asked, his expression tight as if he was annoyed.

"My Lhasa apso. He's old and a little grumpy. He doesn't like it when I stay out late playing with others."

"Your Lhasa apso? You mean Winston is a dog?" He looked so relieved she actually laughed.

"Who did you think he was, my husband?"

"Well... Winston is quite a serious name." He shrugged one shoulder. "How was I to know if you had a sugah daddy waiting at home for you?"

"A sugah daddy? You can't be serious." She let out a throaty laugh. "So, what? You thought I accepted a date with you while my old man was snoring in a recliner at home?"

"Maybe. Hell, how was I supposed to know? And who names their dog Winston?"

"I do," she said primly. "And he's adorable."

"No doubt." He made his way across the parking lot and stopped at a black Mercedes convertible. "Top up or down?"

"Down," she said without hesitation. Her hair was already a bird's nest. It couldn't get much worse.

"You got it." He opened the passenger door and set her in the seat. With one click of a button, the car started and the top automatically folded down. Before she knew it, he was in the driver's seat and they were speeding down the two lane road, heading back into the heart of the village. "Where's your house?"

"Take the next right," she said.

He did as instructed, and soon they were winding their way up the mountain toward her cabin.

Felicia put her hands in the air and let out a whoop

of excitement as he hugged the corners and drove faster than what would be considered a safe speed. It made her feel alive in a way she'd all but forgotten. At her reaction, he sped up even more, driving the car with perfect precision. Every part of her tingled, and by the time the car screeched to a stop in her driveway she felt more live than ever before. "Hot damn that was fun!"

"You're incredible," Christoph said as he scooped her up into his arms again and carried her to the door.

"Why? Because I'm easily impressed by your driving skills?"

"No, because you're not afraid to have a good time."

"I think it's the caffeine talking." She couldn't remember the last time she let herself loose like that. Not without a little liquid courage, anyway. She reached down and opened her front door. Incessant barking came from the back of the house, followed by the *tap, tap, tap* of Winston's nails on her hardwood floor.

Christoph set her down, and she immediately scooped the dog up into her arms and smothered him with kisses. After a moment, she realized Christoph was staring at her, an odd look on his face.

"What?" she asked, placing Winston back on the floor.

He shook his head. "Uh, nothing. Just thinking how lucky Mr. Winston is, that's all."

"Oh." She chuckled and rested a soft hand on his arm. Electricity sparked through her at the contact, and she just stood there for a moment, soaking him in. Crap, had he put a spell on her? How could there be so much chemistry between them? They barely knew each other.

Winston let out a loud bark and ran toward the back of the house. When Felicia didn't acknowledge him, he ran back to her and barked louder.

She glanced down at him and laughed. "I bet you're starving, aren't you boy?" Giving Christoph an apologetic smile, she added, "Give me a few minutes to feed him, then I'll get changed and we can get to work."

"Take your time. I suspect wherever Lemon is, she's probably tucked in for the night. Most people are, unless they're vamps."

"I wouldn't be so sure about that. Not on this island and not when we're talking about Lemon, but it's possible. I'll be right back."

Less than ten minutes later, the dog was fed and Felicia had managed a quick shower. She'd tied her wet hair up into a bun and had swiped on the barest amount of makeup. She wasn't going to win any beauty contests, but she no longer had mud in her cleavage or her hair, and the faint scent of mossy earth had vanished. "Okay. Ready."

He glanced up at her from the couch. Winston was lying on his back in Christoph's lap, soaking up some serious belly rubs.

"How did you do that?" she asked, gesturing to her grumpy old dog. "He hates vampires and men. That's two strikes against you."

"Really? Could've fooled me." Christoph scratched behind the dog's ear, and Winston responded by snuggling in closer. "Maybe I just smell like his mistress."

"I think you're a dog whisperer," she said, her heart melting right on the spot. No one, not even Chad, had charmed her one-woman dog. Christoph had been there less than fifteen minutes, and suddenly they were besties? Either Christoph carried jerky in his pocket, her dog had gone senile, or she'd just hit the jackpot in the man department.

Not that she could keep him. The curse would see to that one way or another. But for the moment, the scene in front of her warmed her icy heart.

"So what's the plan?" Christoph asked, still rubbing Winston's belly.

She couldn't seem to take her mind off the fact that Winston was completely at ease in his lap. "Plan?"

"You said you might know where to start looking for Lemon?" he prompted.

"Lemon, right." She finally lifted her gaze to look him in the eye. "She's a night owl. So even though we don't know where she lives, there are three places to look for her. The bingo hall, the fishing hole, or the recycling warehouse."

"The bingo hall, the fishing hole, or the recycling warehouse? You can't be serious. Is she an eighty-year-old woman trapped in a twenty-seven-year-old body?"

"You know, if she was it would make a hell of a lot of sense." She chuckled. "Come on. This time I drive."

"You think so?" he asked, in a mocking tone.

"I know so." She grabbed his keys that were sitting on the side table and backed up toward the front door. "Are you coming or do you and Winston need some alone time?"

The vampire just chuckled and whispered something to Winston. The dog promptly jumped off his lap and moved to the other end of the couch.

"I knew it! You are a puppy whisperer," she said as he followed her to the door. "I demand you tell me all his secrets. What does he really think of me? Wait, don't answer that. I don't want to know. Just tell me how to keep him from peeing on my bedpost."

"Keep your door closed when you aren't there."

She rolled her eyes, but just laughed as she jumped into the driver's seat without even opening the door. "Come on, faux dog whisperer. You're going to love bingo."

"I doubt it, but if you're there I'm sure it will be interesting."

CHAPTER 8

The car was almost as sexy as Christoph. Felicia gripped the wheel, and for the first time since she'd moved to Witch Island as a kid, she wished the island was bigger; that the roads were straighter and went on for miles. She was dying to open the car up and see what it could really do, but since the island was a maze of narrow, hilly streets, she had to be content with testing the handling and the way it responded to her every command. She could definitely get used to this.

All too soon, she whipped the sexy car into a parking space in front of the Batshit Crazy Bingo Parlor. When she climbed out of the car and turned to Christoph, expecting him to ask about the establishment as every outsider did, she found him studying her, his eyes hooded and his body taught as if he was ready to pounce.

Desire swirled straight to her center, and she sucked in a breath just to settle herself. "You could light someone on fire with that gaze," she said.

"Looks like I already did." He reached over and brushed a lock of hair behind her ear, letting his thumb linger on her jawline.

She couldn't help herself. She leaned into his touch, dying for more contact.

A loud whistle pierced the warm night air, and they both jerked back. "Felicia, is that you in that sexy-ass car?"

She turned, a smile already spreading across her face. "Chad? What the hell are you doing here? I thought you hated bingo."

"It was happy hour. All-you-can-eat wings and two-for-one draft beer. Where else would I be?"

"All-you-can-eat wings? Did you put them out of business?" she asked.

He chuckled. "Almost. They should know better than to run that special with me on the island. I'm the ultimate bottomless pit." Chad turned his attention to Christoph and did a double take. "Hells bells, he's a hottie."

Christoph cleared his throat. "Uh, thanks?"

"Felicia, damn girl. Where'd you find this one?" Chad asked her, still staring at the vampire.

She grinned at her best friend, abandoning any pretense of keeping her cool. "Christoph just walked into the shop this afternoon. And well, here we are."

"At bingo?" he turned to her, horror in his tone.

"Oh, no, sweetheart. How many times have I told you that bingo is not a place to take a date?" He turned to Christoph. "I have to apologize for my friend. She's not very experienced—ouch." He spun and glared at Felicia, who'd elbowed him in the side for telling her date that she was inexperienced. She glared back and gave him her *I can't believe you said that* look.

Sorry, he mouthed and turned back to Christoph. He cleared his throat. "As I was saying, she'd not that experienced at *planning* dates. For whatever reason, she seems to think people actually enjoy this activity. I try to tell her candles, hot oils, wax, nipple clamps, those are all things people enjoy, not coloring a damned bingo card, but some of us are slow learners. Maybe she just needs someone to show her the joys of those nipple clamps first, and then she'll understand. You up for it, Chris?" Chad made a show of glancing at Christoph's crotch. "Looks like you definitely are. Way to go, Fe. Now take him home and get him out of those clothes before someone else does it for you."

"Like you, Chad?" she asked dryly.

"Well..." He raked his gaze over Christoph but then laughed and shook his head. "No way. Jonathon wouldn't take kindly to that." He waved at the man in question standing near the door and chatting with Frankie, the witch who owned the local bookstore. They both waved back then gestured for Chad to join them. "I wouldn't want him to call off the wedding, would I?"

"Wedding?" Felicia squealed. "Did he finally ask

you? Where's the ring? When is it? Do you still want black roses, or have you moved on to something less morose?"

"Calm down, Lassie," he said, patting her head as his eyes twinkled with happiness. "He just asked me last night. I was going to tell you, but by the time I got off work you were already at Witchin' Impossible, and you know how Jonathon feels about me going to that place." He gave Christoph a chagrined smile. "I always get a little crazy when I'm in a room full of mostly naked men. It's like a drug or something. The last time I was there, Cooper had a wardrobe malfunction and the next thing I knew, his frank and beans were in the spotlight. A woman took a picture, and by midnight it had gone viral on social media. Oh man, was he mad. He didn't talk to me for a month."

"Why, were you the one that posted it?" Christoph asked, appearing to be weirdly entertained by the story.

"Oh no, honey. I'm the one who made his banana hammock disappear... by accident, of course."

"Right. Accident," Felicia said, rolling her eyes.

"And how exactly did make his banana hammock disappear?" Christoph somehow managed to ask with a straight face.

"It's my special talent, undressing men." He pumped his eyebrows suggestively at Felicia's date.

"Oh for crying out loud. It's his magic. When he gets overly excited, it malfunctions. That's why Jonathon doesn't let him go to Witchin' Impossible anymore. Besides, the staff started a petition to have him banned after the Cooper incident. No one wants their junk on the internet."

"That wasn't my fault!" Chad insisted. "That woman shoulda been brought up on charges. Of course, Cooper has absolutely nothing to be ashamed of." He leaned in and fake-whispered to Felicia, "You saw his assets, right?"

"Okay, that's enough." Felicia slipped her arm through Chad's and practically dragged him away from Christoph. "What are you trying to do? Run him off?"

"That guy, leaning against that fine-ass car, staring at your ass? Sweetheart, a vampire slayer couldn't run him off. That man is desperate for some Fe-Fe time. You know what I'm sayin'?"

She cast a quick glance over her shoulder and for just a brief second, she caught Christoph's smoldering gaze. When she turned back around, she breathed, "Yes. I think I do."

"Good." Chad stopped, gathered her into a hug, and whispered, "Whatever you do, do not leave that man's side until he's done a thorough body check. Do we understand each other?"

"Yes." She laughed and hugged him back. "Tell Jonathon congratulations and that I expect to see you both in the shop sooner rather than later. No putting this off. I know you two are going to want something special order, and I'm going to have to source it. Which is fine, but I need time, understood?"

He saluted her. "Yes, Major. We'll get right on that."

She kissed his cheek and waved as she walked back

to Christoph. But after she took a few steps, she paused and called over her shoulder, "Hey, have you seen Lemon?"

He frowned. "Mom jeans, crop top, and bad eighties hair?"

"Yeah, that's the one. We need to find her."

"I think she was here earlier for a minute. Or maybe it was over at Ten Thousand and Two Flavors. Jonathon had a hankering for caramel chocolate ribbon with lavender ice cream."

"Jonathon did?" she asked skeptically.

"I might have made the suggestion." His grin widened. "Anyway, it was either here or there." He wrinkled his nose and took on an air of judgement. "She was in acid wash jeans and a mesh crop top, and she had a purple scrunchie in her overly permed hair."

"Sounds about right. Thanks."

"Your friend is—" Christoph started after she returned to the car.

"Overwhelming?" Felicia finished for him.

"I was going to say entertaining. But I could see overwhelming. It sounds like nonstop chatter is normal for him."

"Define normal," she said with a chuckle. Then she shook her head. "No, he isn't always like that. Just when he's excited. Usually when it's just the two of us, we can go hours watching trash television without even saying a word to each other."

"Trash television," he said, nodding. "So, you're good friends then."

"Why do you say that?" Gravel crunched under her feet as they made their way toward the front door.

"Because no one watches trash television with someone who would judge them. Which show?"

"819 Bourbon Street," she said. It was a reality show about a hodgepodge group of paranormals who lived in the heart of the French Quarter.

He laughed. "I should've known. Who's your favorite character?"

"Sabastian. Who else?"

"Ah, the sexy vampire. I think that bodes well for me." He grinned, showing off his fangs.

"Well, in the absence of Sabastian, I think you'll do." She stopped at the front door of the bingo hall. "Do you think you're ready for this?"

"For a place called the Batshit Crazy Bingo Parlor? You bet your pretty ass I am."

"Okay, you asked for it." Chuckling to herself, Felicia pushed the door open and stepped aside. "After you, sir."

He nodded and strode inside.

She waited a few beats until she heard him say, "Holy shit."

Snickering, she followed him in and spotted old man Peterman sitting in his nightshirt and boxers. He had a cigar dangling from his lips as he leered at Mable Mercury, who was wearing a bright pink thong, thigh highs, and a silk camisole.

"Strip senior bingo?" he asked, his eyebrows raised.

She shrugged. "Not always, just every other Friday

night."

"Is that all," he said with a chuckle. "Is that what your friend Chad was doing here? Strip bingo?"

"Chad? Oh, gods no," she said, shaking her head. "He talks a good game, but that man would wear an undershirt in the pool if Jonathon would let him. He's majorly shy when it comes to taking any article of clothing off. It's more likely they were playing Trivia bingo. Things like Famous Porn Stars of the 80s, or Greatest Boy Bands, or Pop Princesses Everyone Loves to Hate."

He nodded. "That makes much more sense."

"Bingo!" Patty Lancaster called as she jumped out of her chair. The entire room gasped as her baggy drawers slipped, and suddenly she was mooning the entire room.

"Someone give me my sunglasses. I'm going blind with all that reflective surface," a friend near her called out.

"It can't be that reflective! Last weigh-in, the doctor said I was five pounds under weight!" Patty shot back and did a hip sashay, not even bothering to pull up her drawers.

"Oh damn, I did not need to see that," her friend shot back.

The older man sitting next to her pulled the woman's glasses off the top of her head and put them on. He peered at Patty and let out a low whistle. "Those cheeks can't be a day older than fifty-eight."

"Hector, are you flirtin' with me?" Patty asked,

finally covering her moon.

"Will it get me a date to the bonfire tomorrow night?"

"It sure will," she said sweetly as she pulled her hippyish cotton skirt on. "Pick me up at nine?"

"I'll be there."

As Patty made her way to the front to collect her winnings, everyone redressed and pulled out new bingo cards. The team of three bartenders stepped out from behind the bar, each of them holding two bottles of high-end vodka. Another team of wait staff appeared and placed shot glasses in front of each of the bingo players.

"Up next is everyone's favorite game. Vodka Bingo. For each number you stamp, take a shot. Our lovely team will keep your glasses filled," the caller announced.

Christoph turned to Felicia. "Is any of this legal?"

"It is on Witch Island," she said, laughing at the fact the senior citizens of her town likely had more fun than a lot of the ladies who frequented Witchin' Impossible. Granted, the bingo parlor didn't have hot men stripping at the moment, but she was willing to bet they were on the agenda for later. Nothing appeared to be out of bounds for Maxi Mabel, the vampire owner of the establishment. Rumor had it she'd once been a dancer at Moulin Rouge in Paris. If so, strip bingo and shot bingo made perfect sense for a vampire in "retirement."

"Oh, is that one going to play with us?" Patty asked,

pointing at Christoph as she made her way back to her seat. "Because if so, I propose we play another round of strip bingo. Or make it a double header, strip and shot bingo."

A collective round of agreement rose up from the women in the room. The men took one look at Christoph and shook their heads, grumbling under their breath.

"Yesssss," a couple of the ladies shouted. One of them stood and ran over to him, grabbing his arm. She tugged him toward her table and said, "You can sit over here, handsome."

Christoph turned to Felicia, panic in his wide eyes. He mouthed, *Help!*

"I don't know what to tell you, handsome," Felicia said, an evil streak taking hold. "Maybe you should play a hand. Give these ladies a chance to see what's under that shirt of yours."

"You mean you want to see what's under this shirt," he hissed.

She shrugged. "I wouldn't complain."

"The moment we leave this building, I'll rip my shirt off for you. Just don't throw me to the wolves. I'm not ready for strip bingo. I'm not even sure I'm ready for regular bingo. Come on, Felicia. Don't leave me hanging here."

His desperate plea made her giggle. She reached out, grabbed his hand, and said, "Sorry, Miss Lancaster, but Christoph and I don't have time for a game. Maybe next time, all right?"

The elder woman let out a disappointed huff. "I suppose you don't have time because you're gonna hog him all to yourself. That's pretty selfish, you know that, right Felicia? You couldn't just let us take a peek at that incredible chest." She let her gaze sweep over Christoph, eyeing him as if she were a starving tiger.

"Well, if I was, that'd be my business, wouldn't it, ma'am?" Felicia said patiently.

"Humph." The older woman plopped back into her chair and asked her friend, "Where were we?"

Her friend pushed a shot of vodka in her direction. "We were just getting ready to get sloshed."

"Right." The woman picked up one of the shot glasses and downed it as if it was something she did every day.

"Time to go," Christoph said, moving toward the door, clearly trying to make a break for it.

She shook her head. "You go on. I'm going to ask if anyone's seen Lemon."

He frowned. "Right. I almost forgot that was why we were here."

She patted his arm. "You have two choices. You can stay here and risk getting accosted again, or you can come with me while I find out if anyone's seen her."

He glanced around, a hint of fear in his eyes as he said, "I'll come with you."

She nodded, clasped her hand in his, and said, "This way. I'll protect you."

"You better."

Ten minutes later, they spilled out of the bingo hall

with Christoph holding his left butt cheek.

"It can't hurt that much," Felicia said. "She's ninety-two years old. How strong could she be?"

"It wasn't just her. It was a dozen of them. Have you ever had your ass pinched by a dozen horny old ladies?"

"No, I can't say that I have," she said through her laughter.

"Then you have no idea what it feels like. I bet I have a cluster of bruises."

She rolled her eyes. "You're a vampire. Your tender buttock isn't bruised."

"It would be if I were human."

She kissed her fingers, then slid her hand down and brushed his away as she gently cupped his perfectly round ass. "Better?"

Desire flashed over his face as he turned to stare at her. "I think maybe another kiss might be just the trick."

She giggled, but kissed the other hand and turned into him so that she could slide it down to his other butt cheek.

"That's it," he said, shifting so that he was pressed up against her body. He was long, hard, and lean, and even though she very much enjoyed cupping his backside, her hands ached to explore everything else he had to offer. "I'm going to kiss you now," he whispered as he bent his head to hers.

"Finally," she whispered back, and rose up on the balls of her feet to meet him halfway.

CHAPTER 9

Felicia tasted of honey and a hint of tart cherries. And the sensation made him want to devour her right there in the parking lot. With one hand buried in her long dark hair, he slid the other one down her side, enjoying her lush curves, nearly driving himself crazy wondering what it would be like to feel her delicate bare skin. Just the thought of her naked beside him made him groan with need.

The sound made her sway in closer and press her delicious body into his. Every inch of her was molded to him, and if they hadn't needed to find that damned witch to save his brother and his best friend's wedding, he'd have taken her back to his hotel right that minute. Or maybe just to the backseat of his rental car. Because dammit, he wanted her. Wanted her more than anyone he'd ever wanted in his life. There was just something about her that drove him insane.

And judging by the groan she let out when she tore herself from him, she was feeling just about the same. The knowledge filled him with a sense of pride, and it was enough to tide him over until he could get her alone. Because he knew now, he would have her. There was no doubt in his mind. The only question was when.

"The fishing hole or the recycling center?" Felicia asked.

"Um, what?" He stared down at her lips in confusion. Was she suggesting a new make out place? All thoughts of looking for Lemon fled as he contemplated kissing her again. "How about that bench over there in the shadows? It's closer."

She frowned then chuckled. "No, you horn dog. We need to keep looking for Lemon."

"Right." He sucked in a breath, trying to calm himself. "Well, which is closer?"

"The recycling center. Come on. You're gonna love it."

He opened the car door for her, shaking his head. He couldn't imagine why he'd be remotely interested in a recycling center, but he hadn't thought bingo was going to be entertaining either. How wrong he was. If he'd lived long enough to be a senior, he'd definitely have wanted to spend his golden years on Witch Island. Who wanted to waste away in a boring home when you could be playing strip bingo?

"What are you smiling at?" she asked.

"You." He hopped into the passenger seat, happy to

let her drive. He loved the intense look she got on her face and the pure joy that streamed from her as she let her guard down. It was sexy as hell and he was here for it. "Come on, let's go find her so we can get back to making out."

She let out a snort of amusement and slammed the car into gear.

~

"When you said recycling center, I thought you meant a place to process glass and cardboard," Christoph said, glancing at the long row of artists' tents. Each one had wares made out of repurposed items—flatware, kitchenware, art pieces, furniture, jewelry, notebooks, sculptures. If one could dream it up, it was probably for sale, made out of the island's garbage. "Is this place open every night?"

"Just on weekends and during special events," Felicia said, taking his hand.

He twined his fingers through hers and started to wonder if he could get away with telecommuting. Did he really need to fly home on Monday? He was the boss of his small investment firm, after all. He'd have to check and see if he had any pressing meetings. If not, he was certain he'd need to extend his stay at the hotel, because he knew he wasn't even remotely ready to leave the dark-haired beauty leading him through the art market.

"Need a hat for the wedding?" she pointed to a rack

of distressed leather hats that had paranormal creatures carved into the material.

He'd seen that type of thing before, but the ones at the recycle market were truly extraordinary. The intricate details of the one he studied made it look as if the dragon was actually in flight. If he stared at it long enough, he could almost see the creature gliding through the air. "Impressive." He picked it up and placed it on his head.

"Oh, monsieur, zee hat, it looks so good on you. Ees perfect, no?" the artist asked Felicia.

"It definitely highlights his good looks," she said with a glint in her eye.

"Sold." Christoph handed the proprietor his credit card.

"Does the gentleman want to see the total?" he asked.

Christoph waved an unconcerned hand. "No. I'll wear it out."

Felicia shook her head. "You know, if you'd negotiated with him, you probably would've gotten a much better deal."

"It was worth it to see your face light up when I told him I'd take it." He slipped his arm around her waist. "Now tell me again how handsome it makes me."

"You're handsome without it," she said. "But, it does add just a little bit of edge. Dark and dangerous. Two traits every bad boy needs on his resume."

He bent his head and lightly scraped his fangs along

her neck. When she shivered in his arms, he added, "You have no idea just how bad I can be."

A small moan escaped from her parted lips, and he longed to kiss her so thoroughly she was forever ruined for anyone else. And judging by the way she was staring at his lips, he guessed she was feeling just about the same. His groin tightened.

"Very well, monsieur. Here's your card and your receipt. I just need your signature."

Christoph barely looked at the price as he signed the ticket. "Thank you," he said. "I think this hat is going to come in quite handy."

"I certainly hope so." The artist retreated back into his space, and Felicia started tugging Christoph down the aisle.

"They have everything from soap to coffins here," she said, pointing to a stall with ornate, gold inlay coffins.

"You know that thing about us vamps sleeping in coffins is just a rumor, right? No one I know sleeps in one of those things. Too dangerous."

"Oh, how so?" she asked, genuine interest in her tone.

"Haven't you ever heard the term 'buried alive?'"

"Sure, but—oh."

He nodded. "Right. People who are intent on ridding the world of vampires usually don't try to stake us. They just wait for their opportunity when we're dead to the world. Do you know how long it takes to dig one's way out of a grave?"

"No. Do you?" she asked, astonished.

"Unfortunately, yes."

She visibly shuttered and tugged him away from the coffin displays. "None of that then. Sorry. I just thought one would be interesting in the front window of my floral shop."

He shrugged. "To everyone other than vampires, I suppose."

"Right. No coffins. What about the soap? Need any supplies?"

Leaning down, he whispered in her ear, "The only supplies I need are a large box of condoms. But I don't think I'll be picking them up at the upcycle place."

"Ewww, definitely not. No."

They were still laughing when they turned the corner. Dark curls caught Christoph's attention, and he paused. Leaning down he said, "Isn't that Lemon over at the place with the fascinators?"

"Fascinators?" she asked, her brow wrinkled.

"Yes, fascinators. The crazy tiny hats the Brits wear? There's a booth of them right over there. See the one made out of soup cans? Princess Maven made that style fashionable just last month."

She stared at him for just a second, and then her lips curved up as her eyes twinkled in amusement. "You keep up with the royals' fashion choices?"

"Not exactly." He rocked back on his heels, feeling chagrined that he was up on tabloid gossip. "It's just hard to escape when you're in London."

"Is that where you were before you came here?" she

asked, appearing to forget all about the Lemon sighting.

"Felicia," he said, shaking his head slightly. "I'll tell you all about it… later. Right now we have a witch to speak to." He nodded his head toward the tent.

"Oh! Right." She spun around, but not before he saw the blush creep over her cheeks.

He couldn't stop the warm feeling that blossomed in his chest. She was interested. There was no doubt about it.

CHAPTER 10

Snap out of it, Felicia, she told herself as she eyed Lemon trying on a half dozen ridiculous hats that couldn't block out a ray of sunshine even if they tried. She was far too invested in Christoph. Liked him more than she should. Because already she knew it was going to suck hard when he got on that plane on Monday. *But it's only Friday,* the helpful voice in the back of her mind said. *Enjoy it while you can.*

She was certainly going to try. But not until after they fixed the Jasper and Bianca situation. Still holding Christoph's hand, Felicia led him over to the stall where Lemon was admiring herself in a small hand mirror. Her look was nothing short of insane. She still wore her acid wash jeans and mesh crop top, but she'd changed her shoes and was now wearing leopard print, impossibly high designer heels. And the hat she'd chosen was steampunk, complete with a working clock sticking out of the top. It was too much for Felicia's eyes to process. She blinked and when she focused again, Lemon was gone.

"Where'd she go?" she asked Christoph as she glanced around.

"I have no idea," he said, not bothering to hide his frustration. "One second she was there trying on that crazy hat, then she spotted you and literally vanished into thin air."

"Are you kidding?" Is that what had happened earlier at Witchin' Impossible? Did Lemon have the skill to just disappear? Was she teleporting, or just finding a way to go invisible? Felicia rushed forward, her arms out, speculating that if Lemon was still in solid form, she might run into her.

"Ma'am, you're blocking the aisle," an older man pushing a cart of handmade sheet metal instruments said. He had everything from guitars to harps on the flatbed.

"Sorry." She quickly brought her arms back to her sides and let out a frustrated sigh.

"Whatever it is, love, I'm sure it will work out," the woman at the booth said.

"I hope so." Felicia leaned against the woman's table and glanced around at the fun hats. She picked up one that had a unicorn head sticking out the top.

"It's for that unique person who's one of a kind," the artist said. "And a great defensive weapon," she joked.

Felicia gently pressed the tip of her finger to the

unicorn horn and nodded. "Definitely. One could poke an eye out." She placed the hat back on its stand. "Very fun, but I think I better stick to something a little less… accident prone."

"This one suits you." The artist picked up a green felted hat that had sunflowers embroidered all over it.

"You have no idea just how much," Christoph said, handing the vendor his credit card. "We'll take it."

"Christoph," Felicia said. "This isn't necessary. When am I going to wear that?"

He leaned in, pressed a soft kiss just below her ear, and said, "Later tonight when I finally manage to deflower you."

"Right," she breathed, welcoming the familiar need building at her center. "Later can't come soon enough." She pressed her hands on the table just to keep from grabbing Christoph and leaned forward. "Listen, you know that woman who was here just a minute ago—" A shiny gold locket lying in the middle of the table caught Felicia's eye.

"The one with acid wash jeans?" the artist managed to say with a straight face.

"The one and only," Christoph confirmed.

"Is this yours?" Felicia picked up the locket, holding it in front of the artist. Before she could answer, Felicia already knew Esmerelda was the owner. Her cousin had been there. And it had to be in the recent past because her energy was still crawling all over the necklace.

"No. I think the woman you're looking for was

wearing it though. It must've fallen off while she was trying on the fascinators."

"Lemon?" She turned to Christoph, a combination of excitement and fear running through her. "Lemon has seen my cousin."

"Okay," he said. "So?"

"My cousin has been missing for ten years." She grabbed him by the shirt and yanked him out of the aisle. "We have to go now. Her energy is still fresh on the locket. If we move quickly, I can use a tracking spell to find her."

"Who? Lemon?"

'No. My cousin Esme," she said.

"But what about Bianca and Jasper?"

"Dammit." She knew it was selfish to run off and track down her cousin when there was a wedding to save, but she'd waited years for this. She couldn't pass up the opportunity now. "We'll keep looking after we find Esme. This is important, Christoph. Besides, Lemon was wearing this. Maybe my cousin has an idea of where to find her."

He slipped his hand back into hers and said, "Okay. We can spare a few minutes to find your missing cousin." His smile was gentle as he squeezed her fingers. "Shall we?"

"We shall." Then she turned on her heel and hurried back to the Mercedes.

THE ENERGY ON THE LOCKET WAS STRONG. SO STRONG that Felicia wondered how it was possible that Lemon had been the one wearing it. Surely the fresh contact would've dulled her cousin's energy and infused a touch of Lemon's. But it certainly didn't feel that way. It was so fused with Esmerelda's energy that she hadn't even needed to cast a tracking spell. Esme's energy just kept getting stronger and stronger as they headed toward the Fishing Hole. It was the third place Felicia had marked to search for Lemon, but it looked like she was going to find someone else instead.

Nerves unsettled her stomach, and Felicia found it a little hard to breathe. What would she say to the person who had cursed her very happiness and then run off? One thing was for sure; she was certain a few choice swear words would be involved.

But she didn't just want to see Esme because she was angry. She wanted to hug her, slug her, and cast a spell that put boils on her ass for a month. And most of all, she just wanted to make sure the woman who'd been her best friend was all right.

"You're quiet over there," Christoph said from the driver's seat.

"I'm just thinking. It's been a long time since I've seen her." She glanced out into the night, the pull of Esme's presence reverberating from the locket clutched in her hand.

Christoph placed a comforting hand on her knee. "I'm sure she'll be really happy to see you, too."

Felicia couldn't help it. She let out a snort of laughter. "I guess we'll find out."

He frowned and opened his mouth to ask her something, but she pointed to his left.

"That's the Fishing Hole."

He glanced over at the seaside cove where twinkle lights lit up the beach. Individual luxury cabins dotted the seashore, and there were a half dozen campfires flickering in the darkness. Off to the right, a group of people stripped down to their birthday suits and ran, shrieking with delight into the water. "Please tell me the seniors don't hang out here after strip bingo?"

"Definitely not. They reserve the place on Wednesdays for their Polar Bear Club activities."

He groaned and she laughed.

"Gotta love 'em. They sure do know how to have a good time."

Christoph steered the car around a tight turn, leaving the Fishing Hole behind him. "Are we close?"

"I think so. The pull is to the left, so I'm guessing the next road you come to, make the turn."

"You got it." Without warning he jerked on the steering wheel and made a turn.

Felicia let out a gasp of surprise as they rumbled onto a bumpy dirt road she hadn't even known existed. "Where the hell did that turn come from?"

He shrugged one shoulder. "Is it the right way?"

Felicia's connection to Esme grew so strong, she could almost smell Esme's lavender scent. "Definitely. Stop the car."

He did as she asked and killed the engine. Neither of them used the door as they climbed out, preferring instead to make the least amount of noise as possible.

Felicia didn't have any idea if Esme wanted to see her. If she did, couldn't she have just come to her house or shop? It wasn't as if she was hard to find on the island. Hell, even her phone number was the same. Considering Esme hadn't made an effort, Felicia had to assume seeing her cousin wasn't on her agenda.

Well, too damned bad, Felicia thought. It was high time Esmerelda faced her cousin and rectified the reckless spell she'd cast on her ten years ago. Felicia's heart hammered against her ribcage. For the first time in what felt like a lifetime, she let herself think about what her life might be like if the spell was neutralized. A husband? Kids? Grandkids? Was any of it possible? She glanced at Christoph. Could he possibly be the one? Paranormal medical breakthroughs had been made in recent years, making it possible for vampires to sire children. If he was the one and they decided they wanted kids, they'd have options. Every possibility would be laid at her feet.

Her head spun with the idea. But then she shook herself. The scenario she'd just conjured up in her mind was pure fantasy. Vampires rarely got married. That forever thing, it really spooked them. And they'd literally just met. If he knew she was conjuring up happily-ever-afters in her mind, he'd be running for the next plane off the island. She probably would too if some guy she'd just met started talking about marriage and kids.

But what if he started talking about a family? Would it freak her out? As she gazed at his profile, she really didn't think so. Strange. Why was she so damned comfortable with him?

"Up ahead," Christoph said under his breath. "Is that... Lemon?"

Felicia squinted at the person pacing in front of a broken-down shack. It looked a little like the ones over at the Fishing Hole, only this one had a sagging roof and boarded up windows. "What is she doing?"

He turned his head, listening intently. "It sounds like she's arguing with herself. Something about how she never should've left the cabin tonight."

"She's not wrong," Felicia said dryly. If she hadn't, Felicia probably would've been in bed with Christoph right that minute, experiencing the orgasm of her life. Or would she? Would the curse have reared its ugly head again and found another way to keep her and the vampire apart? It was likely.

"At least we found her," Christoph said. "Want me to talk to her while you find your cousin?"

Felicia started to nod but then frowned. The energy in the locket was pulling her straight toward Lemon. How in the world was that possible? It was time to confront the troublemaking witch. "No, we can talk to her together."

"Okay." Christoph gestured for her to take the lead on the small path that led to the cabin.

With each step she took, the locket grew warmer and warmer, until Felicia was forced to open her hand or risk being branded by the hot metal. The moment she opened her fist, the necklace flew out of her hand, straight toward Lemon.

"Oh my goddess!" Felicia gasped out.

Lemon's head snapped up, and magic flickered all over her body as she started to fade into the ether.

"No!" Felicia raised a hand, and magic streamed from her, coiling like a rope around Lemon—make that Esmerelda. The moment Felicia's magic touched the other woman, the bad fashion and outdated perm faded away, leaving a petite beauty in her place. "Esme," Felicia said, shaking her head. "This is where you've been all these years?"

Esme struggled against her magical restraints. "Let me go!"

"Oh, I don't think so," Felicia said, stalking over to her cousin. "Not after the heartache you've caused. What is the matter with you?"

Esmerelda clamped her mouth shut and glanced away as if unable to look her cousin in the eye.

"Don't think for a second I'm leaving until we get some answers."

Esmerelda sucked in a deep breath and blew it out, then turned defeated eyes on Felicia. "There's nothing to talk about, Fe. What's done is done, and once again, I'm the odd woman out."

"What are you talking about?" Felicia glanced at

Christoph. He raised his hands in a helpless motion. He didn't have a clue either.

"You got Chad. That vampire woman got Jasper. And what do I get? Pretending to be Lemon while she's off in Paris being an artist in residence at one of the most prestigious art houses in the city."

"Whoa. Wait. Lemon is in Paris... pretending to be an artist?"

Esmerelda shook her head. "Not pretending. She *is* being an artist. We traded places. She's me and I'm her for the next six months."

"You're an artist?" Felicia asked, completely confused.

"I was an artist. Now I'm just a crazy islander who keeps to herself so I can spy on my ex and the cousin who hates me."

"You're spying on Chad?" Felicia needed to sit down. Or have Esme draw her a picture because she just wasn't getting it.

"No. Not Chad. Jasper." She tried to throw her hands up in the air, but Felicia's magic stopped her. Then tears started to fall silently down her cheeks.

Felicia's first instinct was to go to her cousin and console her, but she stayed perfectly still, unwilling to fall for anymore of her tricks.

"You cursed Jasper?" Christoph asked. "Why?"

"Because he was supposed to love me, not Vampire Barbie," she spat out.

"That's uncalled for." Christoph said in an icy tone. "Bianca hasn't done anything to you, but I'm guessing you're the reason she almost went into a blood-loss coma earlier this evening."

"Coma?" she echoed as her voice cracked. "That wasn't... I didn't mean... I just wanted them to fight so he'd come back to me."

"You've got to be kidding me!" Felicia shouted, suddenly losing her self-control. "It's been ten years, and you're still attacking other women because your own relationships didn't work out. What is wrong with you?"

Esme's face went white, and although she couldn't walk away because Felicia's magic held her in place, she was able to turn her head and hide her face behind her long mane of blond hair.

"She did this before?" Christoph asked Felicia.

"Yeah." She let out a humorless laugh. "To me, all because my best friend dumped her for another man."

"Another man?" Esme and Christoph both said at the same time.

"That's right, Esme. You cursed me to a life of loneliness because Chad lied to you. He was never in love with me. It was Jonathon and he was too afraid to tell you." Felicia snorted. "I can't imagine why. Look at how well you take breakups. What did Jasper do to you? Promise you the moon then take it back when he decided he was in love with Bianca?"

"No! He didn't offer me the moon. He offered to marry me. To turn me into a vampire. We spent a perfect summer together in Paris. Then he left and said he'd be back in the spring. But he never showed up. I spent six months pining for him. Imagine my surprise when I found out he was marrying *her* in my home town. He hurt me. All I wanted to do was hurt him back."

Felicia and Christoph shared a glance. He cleared his throat. "She cursed you to a life of loneliness? What does that mean exactly?"

She sighed. "Just that none of my relationships work out. They are all doomed to implode."

A strange look crossed his features. Then he marched over to Esme and grabbed her by the arm. Felicia's magic disappeared, and he started hauling her down the trail.

"Get your cold dead hands off me," she ordered.

"I don't think so," he said. "Not until your magic is neutralized."

"What? No. You can't do this to me. I'll sue." She tried to dig her heels into the sand, but it was no use. Christoph pulled her along as if she weighed nothing.

Felicia let out a small huff of laughter. "Seems we both have litigious family members."

Christoph shrugged. "Go for it. My lawyers will bury you. And if we end up pressing criminal charges, just think how much fun it will be in the supernatural jail out there on Rock Island. I hear it snows more than half the year there. Sounds pleasant, doesn't it?"

"Criminal charges?" she whimpered.

"You did curse my brother and maybe the vampire that attacked Bianca. An unauthorized curse. Add in

Felicia's testimony, and I think a jury probably isn't going to take kindly to your petty jealousy."

Thick tears rolled down Esme's face. "I didn't mean to hurt anyone. I just..." She sniffed and turned her pleading gaze on Felicia. "I don't know what came over me."

"I do," Felicia said. "Just get in the car. And if you so much as even move a muscle wrong, you'll regret it, understand?"

She nodded.

"Good. Now get in the back seat." Felicia kept an eagle eye on her cousin, not trusting her in the slightest. Once she was buckled in the back, Felicia climbed in beside her and wrapped a lose coil of magic around her wrists. "If you try to escape, I'll tighten my magic so firmly you'll have trouble breathing, got it?"

More tears fell down Esme's face, but she gave Felicia a short nod. Then she shifted, staring at the sea.

"You okay?" Christoph asked Felicia.

"Okay as I'm gonna be. Can you take us to the healer?"

"Sure. Where's the office?" he asked as he climbed into the driver's seat.

She gave him a grateful smile. "Right next to Witchin' Impossible."

"Seriously? Is it a rehydration clinic or something?"

Felicia laughed as she recalled reading about mobile clinics that set up shop in party towns to help people recover from hangovers faster. Painkillers combined with an IV to combat dehydration drew big money in place like New Orleans and Las Vegas. But on Witch Island? An over indulger could expect to get laughed at, not offered a reprieve in the form of medical care. "Not even close. Mystia is a little judgmental about the partiers that frequent that establishment. For the most part, she figures they get what they deserve."

"She's probably right," he agreed and glanced at Esmerelda in the rear view mirror. She was certain he was thinking the same thing about her cousin. What would happen to her now? Felicia had no idea. But she did know Esme needed help, and Mystia was the person to ask.

CHAPTER 11

Mystia's adorable gothic home and office was dark except for the one porch light. Next to the door, there was a glowing yellow button that everyone on the island knew was only for emergencies. Felicia hesitated for just a moment but then pressed it. As far as she was concerned, her cousin's mental state was a danger to society. And Felicia knew she wasn't equipped to keep her out of trouble. It was way past time for a professional to step in.

The door swung open, and Mystia stood in the darkened entry, her eyes puffy from sleep and a frown on her face. She took one look at Felicia and said, "If this could've waited until the morning then I'm charging double."

"I'll pay double anyway," Christoph said, giving her a nod. "Can we come in?"

Mystia glanced at the magic still encircling Esmerelda's wrists and said, "I guess you'd better."

A light flickered on, illuminating a cozy sitting room. Mystia waved a hand at the couch. "Take a seat."

"Is everything all right?" a familiar male voice sounded from the hallway.

Felicia glanced up and spotted Cooper. "Hey, you okay?"

His eyes narrowed as he focused on Esmerelda. "Don't I know you?"

"No," she said thickly. "Not really. No one does."

She sounded so pathetic that Felicia didn't know if she should feel sorry for her or be annoyed. The woman had brought all of this on herself after all. "She's the one who cursed Bradley and Jasper."

She jerked her head and stared at me. "Who's Bradley?"

"Goddess above. You don't even know who you cursed. Are you that clueless?"

She clamped her mouth shut and stared straight ahead.

Felicia rolled her eyes. "He's the vampire who attacked Bianca. Are you saying you didn't curse him?"

Esmerelda didn't respond.

"I'll take that as a yes." She turned her attention to Cooper and touched her neck. "Did you heal up okay?"

His gaze flickered to Mystia as he nodded, pride gleaming in his eyes. "My girl can do amazing things."

"I'm not your girl," Mystia said, pulling a syringe out of her healer bag.

"So you keep telling me," he said good naturedly. "But you don't seem to have a problem with sleepovers."

Mystia gave him a withering glare. He just laughed and nodded to Felicia. "I'm fine. You?"

"I will be just as soon as my cousin here gets some real help."

"I don't need any help," Esmerelda said stubbornly.

"The hell you don't," Cooper said. "Anyone who goes around cursing people, no matter what the reason is, could probably use some psychotherapy."

"Okay, that's enough armchair diagnoses," Mystia said. "Cooper, make yourself scarce or you'll have to sleep in your own bed tonight."

"Got it," he said and promptly retreated up the long narrow stairway. When he got to the top of the landing, he turned and waved at Felicia and mouthed *Good luck.*

Felicia nodded to Mystia and mouthed the same thing back to him.

He chuckled and disappeared into the dark hallway.

"Okay," Mystia said as she dabbed a bit of rubbing alcohol onto to a cotton ball and moved to Esmerelda's side. "This is just a vitamin boost. I can tell by the energy you're putting out that your system is running on fumes. Don't worry. You'll barely feel a thing."

Esmeralda flinched away, but Mystia was too quick for her. Without missing a beat, she grabbed her arm, swabbed her skin, and then plunged the needle into her shoulder.

Felicia was impressed. Mystia had done that a time or two before.

"Now," Mystia said. "Who's going to tell me about this curse?"

Felicia and Christoph both turned their gazes on Esmerelda.

"I never meant to hurt anyone," she whimpered as the color brightened in her cheeks.

Felicia let out an exasperated sigh. "You already know about what happened at Witchin' Impossible. I don't know how Bradley is involved, but Esme has already confessed to cursing Jasper. She just wanted him to bite someone so Bianca would leave him."

"Is it a permanent curse?" she asked Esmerelda.

Felicia's cousin gave her a half shrug. "It's not supposed to be."

"And Bradley? How does he play into this?"

Still staring blankly at the wall, she said, "He was just a bystander. Jasper was talking to him when I unleashed the curse."

"I see. Then it was just a lucky coincidence for you that he ended up biting Bianca." It wasn't a question.

Esmerelda nodded anyway. "Like I said, I wasn't trying to physically harm anyone."

The healer picked up her phone and dialed. "Bradley, can you come down here, please?"

Felicia's eyes widened as she realized the vampire in question was on the premises.

Esmerelda recoiled. "He's here?"

"He was recovering from his episode and was

disoriented," Mystia said, her tone neutral. Felicia was impressed with her professionalism because she knew Mystia well enough to understand that the healer had strong feelings about what Esme had done.

Heavy footsteps sounded on the stairs. Bradley appeared, and even in the soft light Felicia could see the dark circles rimming his eyes. His face was pinched, and there was no denying the heavy presence of guilt clinging to him. When he spotted Christoph, he paused. "What's going on? Is Bianca all right?"

"As far as I know," Christoph said, leaning back into the couch. "Are you?"

"I…" He shook his head. "I really don't know, to be honest."

Felicia's heart ached for him. Bradley was such a good guy. Knowing that he attacked two of his fellow vampires was probably eating him alive.

"Physically, Mr. Dennison should make a full recovery," Mystia said. "I'd like to test a few things to make sure the spell really has run its course, but for his peace of mind, he needs to hear exactly what happened from the witch who cursed him."

"So I *was* cursed then?" Bradley asked, his eyes flickering over Felicia and then Esmerelda. "Who *are* you?" he asked the latter. "Didn't I see you this afternoon at Jasper's hotel?"

She nodded but didn't offer any additional information.

"She's my cousin," Felicia said. "And she's here to apologize to you. Right, Esme?"

"Um, I guess." She cleared her throat and quietly told him why she'd cursed Jasper. She ended with, "I didn't mean to curse you. You were just an unfortunate bystander. I know the entire thing was wrong, and all I can say is that I'm sorry."

Bradley stared at her for a few beats then shook his head. "You did all of that over Jasper? He's a cool dude and all, but unless he has a magic schlong, then I just don't get it."

Christoph snickered.

"Don't be crass," Esmerelda said quietly.

Felicia tsked. "He can say whatever he wants. You cursed the man."

Bradley slumped down into the chair next to Mystia. "Now what? Does this curse have any lasting effects?"

"That's what we're about to find out." The healer put her notebook down and held one hand out to Bradley and the other to Esmerelda.

Bradley immediately took her hand, but Esmerelda hesitated.

"It would behoove you to cooperate, Ms.…?" Mystia paused, waiting for Esme's response.

"Patterson," Felicia supplied when Esme kept quiet.

Mystia nodded and stared Esme in the eye. "Right, well then, Ms. Patterson, I do believe you're already in enough trouble as it is."

That feral expression suddenly flashed in Esme's eyes again as magic rippled under her skin.

"Esme, no!" Felicia jumped up, certain that Esme

was trying to disappear again. She called up her own magic, but just as the spark hit her fingertips, it winked out. She felt empty, like a heavy cloak covered her skin and the magic was trapped within. "What was that?" she asked Mystia.

"This is a magic free zone," she said, giving Felicia a wan smile. "There is no need to worry. Your cousin isn't going anywhere anytime soon."

Esmerelda let out a cry of frustration as Felicia sat down next to Christoph, relief rushing through her. Christoph took her hand in his and gently traced the back of her hand with his thumb.

"Thank the gods." Felicia nodded her appreciation to Mystia and started to understand why Cooper was attracted to her. The woman was quietly fierce and full of integrity. When this was all over, she was going to make a point of befriending her. She could use more good witches in her life.

"Your hand, Ms. Patterson?" Mystia raised a questioning eyebrow. "Or would you like me to call the authorities?"

Esmerelda reluctantly offered the healer her hand. Mystia sat quietly with her eyes closed as she analyzed the connection between Esme and Bradley. Finally, she let go and smiled softly at Bradley. "Good news. It was just temporary. I'm still sensing a small amount of her magic clinging to you, but it should be gone within a few days. Just lay low for the next forty-eight hours. Absolutely no alcohol of any kind. If you need to take any medication, call me first. By Monday you should be back to normal."

The gloom that had been clinging to Bradley vanished, and the happy go-lucky guy instantly returned with his lopsided grin. "Thank the gods." He turned to Esmerelda. "Listen, I'm not at all okay with the fact that you cursed me," he said earnestly, but gently. "What happened tonight could've ruined more than just one life. I understand that what you did came from a place of pain. I hope you figure out a way to heal and move forward. To love yourself first, before you put your love into another."

"He hurt me," she said weakly.

"No doubt. But does that mean you need to hurt others? Look inside yourself and try to be the person you want to spend the rest of your life with."

She didn't answer as two fat tears rolled down her cheeks.

Bradley stood, shook Mystia's hand, and said, "Thank you. I'm going to head out now. If I hurry, I might still be able to catch the next plane out of here to Aspen. I hear the slopes are full of fresh powder."

"I said to take it easy," she said.

"I will. Trust me. Right up next to the fireplace with the snow bunnies. Then I'll hit the slopes in a few days." He winked, thanked Felicia and Christoph, and disappeared into the night.

"I guess this means Jasper isn't permanently affected either?" Christoph asked.

"I think it's safe to assume as much," Mystia said. "He might want to come in for a once-over though."

Christoph stood. "I think I should let him and Bianca both know about this development." He glanced at Felicia. "Unless you need me to stay."

She shook her head. "No. Go on. Esmerelda and I have some unfinished business to take care of. See you tomorrow at the wedding—assuming you're successful in reuniting the bride and groom of course."

"Definitely. Save a dance for me, all right?"

She nodded.

He leaned down and kissed her on the cheek. "Call me if you need anything."

"Sure."

"I mean it. Anything at all," he said suggestively.

She laughed. "Just go. Fix the rift between Jasper and Bianca." She glanced at the wall clock and winced. It was past two o'clock. At some point she was going to need some sleep if she hoped to have any energy left over for the wedding flowers. "Get some rest so you're ready for tomorrow night."

Mischief sparked in his twinkling eyes. "I'll be ready. Don't you worry about that. The question is, will you?"

Yes. The answer was definitely yes.

CHAPTER 12

"You two seem... cozy," Esmerelda said once Christoph was gone.

"No thanks to you," Felicia shot back.

She turned away again, guilt etched all over her once-pretty face. "I didn't... Dammit!" Jerking back around, she said, "It was a mistake, okay? I didn't mean to curse you. It's not like I planned it. But Chad ripped my heart out, and when he said he was in love with you, I snapped. I had it in my head that you two had been together the whole time; that I'd been made a fool. Nothing you could've said would've gotten through to me. And then we were fighting... full-on fighting right where I was supposed to be getting married that day. I don't know what happened. I lost my mind. The spell just came out of nowhere and the next thing I knew, I was on a plane heading for Europe."

"You just left me there in the rose bushes and got on a plane for Europe. Do you have any idea how fucked-up that is?" Felicia asked, incredulous.

"The rose bushes?" Esme asked, her face full of confusion.

Felicia just shook her head. "You didn't even stop to find out what happened to me. How selfish are you? I loved you, and all you cared about was yourself."

"That's not... I—" A sob got caught in Esme's throat and she stared at Mystia helplessly.

The healer cleared her throat. "I think someone needs to start at the beginning."

Esme shook her head, unable to speak.

"For god's sake." Felicia stood and paced as she told Mystia the entire story. When she was finished, she added, "So here we are. Esme is still cursing people because life hasn't gone her way, and I'm doomed to live a life alone because Chad couldn't be honest with himself or his fiancée. Not that I'm blaming him. This is on her. He had his own demons to battle."

"I see." Mystia scribbled something in her notebook. "And if I'm understanding correctly, Esmerelda, you don't remember anything after you cursed your cousin?"

She shook her head. "It was like I blacked out after the curse. I can't recall leaving the clearing or the island. All I know is that I had my passport clutched in my hand and the plane was headed for London."

Mystia nodded. "And Felicia, tell me about your attempted relationships. What is the normal pattern?"

Felicia let out a humorless snort. "The pattern? Someone comes to town. We hit it off, make plans, have a few dates and as soon as any talk about long-range plans comes into play, all hell breaks loose. Mysterious illnesses, broken bones, family emergencies. Once, a hurricane came out of nowhere. The bride and groom still managed to get married, but my date was trapped in his hotel due to flood waters. His house on the mainland was destroyed, and after he left to deal with the destruction, I never heard from him again. At some point, I just gave up."

"Until Christoph came to town," she said.

Felicia shrugged. "I wasn't expecting it to turn into anything more than a weekend fling. A girl needs some companionship."

Mystia chuckled. "A girl certainly does." She sobered and turned to Esmerelda. "Is this really what you want for your cousin?"

"No!" she said emphatically. "I was just so hurt and depressed. And to be honest, I had no idea it was permanent. How could I know? I was too embarrassed and ashamed to come back here. The first time I stepped back onto the island was last week. I didn't know until tonight that my spell was still in effect. That's never happened before."

"Are you saying that's not the only time you've used that spell?" Mystia asked.

"No. No!" She stood, her fists clenched in frustration. "I don't even know if I could do it again. It was born out of pure anger. I'm saying that the spells

I've cast have always been temporary. Like the one I cast on Jasper. It's already faded."

Mystia nodded and made another note.

"None of that makes what you did to me okay," Felicia said quietly, exhaustion taking over.

"Of course it doesn't," her cousin said, turning apologetic eyes on her. "I was just trying to explain that I didn't understand the ramifications."

"Are you ready to reverse it?" Mystia asked her.

She nodded. "Yes, absolutely. But I don't know how to do that."

Mystia stood. "Luckily, I can help. This way."

Felicia waited for Esmerelda to fall into step behind the healer, and then she followed them into a circular room. Books lined the walls, and sitting in the center of the room was a table with a pentacle carved in the middle.

"Have a seat," she said. "Sit across from one another."

They did as they were told.

"Now clasp hands."

Felicia had been expecting the order and reached out for her cousin. But Esme hesitated. "I'm not going to bite you," Felicia said, irritated.

"It's not that," Esme said, shaking her head. "I just... I'm afraid of it. The magic. The spell. I didn't ever again want to feel what I felt that day."

Felicia just gave her a flat stare.

"Esmerelda," Mystia said. "Can you imagine what it's felt like for Felicia for the last ten years?"

Esmeralda blanched and slowly reached out to take Felicia's hands.

"Good," Mystia said. "Now, both of you close your eyes."

Felicia squeezed her eyes tight and tried not to get her hopes up that today would be the end of the decade-long nightmare. Magic tingled across her skin, warm, inviting magic that most witches craved. Felicia opened her senses and let the magic pour into her. It filled her up, comforted her, made her feel completely safe.

Esme let out a small, tortured moan.

Felicia frowned, but didn't open her eyes. She concentrated on Mystia's magic, letting herself enjoy the sensation.

"It's... awful. Is this what I did?" Esmerelda whimpered. "I can't... I'm so sorry, Felicia. So, so sorry."

Felicia tried to open her eyes, but couldn't. They were sealed shut, and she was unable to move while trapped in her own personal haven.

"Embrace your past, Esmerelda. It's the only way to heal, the only way to let go," Mystia said.

"It hurts too much," she said, her voice faint and far away.

"It'll be over just as soon as you come to terms with your actions."

A cry sounded from her cousin, making Felicia wince.

"Relax, Felicia," Mystia soothed. "It'll be over soon."

Only Felicia couldn't relax, couldn't sit there while her cousin was in pain while she felt like she was at some spa retreat. But what could she do? She was trapped in the magical cocoon.

"I'm so sorry, so, so sorry," Esmerelda said over and over and over again, her cries becoming more and more desperate with each uttered word.

Felicia's heart cracked. Esmerelda had been broken ten years ago when she'd cursed her, and her heart had never healed. And likely never would unless she could find a way to forgive herself. She didn't know if her cousin was strong enough to do that, but Felicia knew she was. She concentrated and was able to tighten her grip on Esme's hands and forced out, "Let it go, Esme. I forgive you. It's over. We can move on from this. I promise."

The magic intensified, warming Felicia's skin. Her eyes flew open just as a bolt of magic crackled across the room and exploded into tiny little sunbursts of light.

Esmerelda let out a long, relieved sigh and sat back in her chair. The stress in her brow had vanished, and her dull blue eyes had brightened. She met Felicia's gaze and gave her a small, shy smile. "Thank you," she whispered.

Felicia smiled back. "You're welcome."

"Where do we go from here?" Felicia asked Mystia once they were back in her cozy sitting room.

She glanced over at Esmerelda who was curled up at the end of the couch, drinking a cup of tea. "I have no choice but to call the authorities."

Felicia sucked in a sharp breath. She knew better than anyone the trouble that Esme's actions had caused, but that didn't mean she wanted to see her cousin in witches jail.

"I'm bound by my oath," she said. "But try not to worry. Your cousin was in trauma when she cast those spells. Both of them. It's my belief that coming back here triggered another episode. It's highly likely that she'll be sentenced to therapy rather than incarceration. It's really the best thing for her."

Felicia met Esme's gaze.

Her cousin gave her a small nod. "It's the right thing, Fe. Whatever comes, I'm ready to handle it now."

With her cousin's words, something deep inside of Felicia settled. Finally, for the first time in a decade, she believed that everything was going to be okay.

CHAPTER 13

The moon shone down on the cobbled streets of Witch Island as Felicia made her way back to her little cottage on the hill. After walking back to her floral shop and picking up her small SUV, she'd quickly headed home, dreaming of cuddling up with Winston for a few hours of sleep before heading back into work.

But when she stumbled out of her car, she stopped dead in her tracks as she spotted Christoph sitting patiently on her steps. He was leaning against the porch railing, his hands clasped in front of him, a small smile curving his lips.

He stood and walked over to her. "Surprise."

"You can say that again. Is everything all right with the bride and groom?"

"Yep." He slipped his arms around her waist and pulled her in close. "Not even thirty minutes ago, the love birds shoved me out of their bridal suite and locked the door. I think they're planning a nice long makeup session."

"Good. That's really excellent." She reached up and slid her arms around his neck. "And you're here because…?"

"I think you know the answer to that." His voice was husky and already full of need.

"To snuggle Winston?" she teased.

"As appealing as that sounds, that's not exactly what I had in mind." He bent his head and brushed his lips over the pulse in her neck.

Her breathing hitched. "So you're saying you came over for… breakfast?"

He chuckled. His breath danced over her skin, sending a tantalizing shiver straight to her toes. "I was thinking more like dessert, but if we end up breaking out the maple syrup, then we can call it breakfast if you like."

"I think there's some in my pantry," she said, closing her eyes as he ran his hands up and over her curves.

"Good. We'll find that later. Much later." He brushed one thumb over her bottom lip and stared into her eyes. His voice rasped as he asked, "Before we start this, I need to know something."

She tensed, startled out of her lust haze. "What's that?"

"Are you all right? After everything that happened tonight with your cousin, are you sure you want me here?"

His question was so earnest and sincere tears burned the backs of her eyes. But she sucked in a calming breath and blinked them back. "Actually, Christoph, to tell you the truth, I'm better than I have been in years. Mystia… she helped to reverse the curse and is getting my cousin help. So the fact that you're here right now, I think it only proves that the curse is in fact broken." Then she grinned, fisted her hand in his shirt, pulled him in close, and whispered, "Which means, if you try to leave, I'm going to do everything in my power to stop you."

He let out a low chuckle. "Don't you worry about that, gorgeous. Right now, my entire world revolves around you and getting you out of those jeans."

"Good. Now shut up and kiss me."

His eyes glinted as he leaned down and gently brushed his lips over hers. He was so sweet, so tender, that Felicia's entire body started to tremble with pure emotion. And when his tongue finally tasted hers, she opened to him, letting him have all of her.

"You taste just like cherries," he whispered, holding her so close, she was molded to him. "Like perfection."

She smiled against his lips and ran a hand over his stubbled jaw. The moonlight illuminated his sexy scruff, and she suddenly wondered what it would feel like with his beard scraping along the inside of her thigh. "Oh, goddess," she said, her knees weakening with the thought.

He pulled back for just a moment, one eyebrow

going up as he watched her. "I'm not sure what I did to illicit that response. Care to share so I can do it again?"

Heat filled her cheeks as she trailed her fingers over his jaw again. "I was just… um, anticipating."

Recognition lit his intense gaze and was immediately replaced with something that resembled determination. "I see. Well, don't let me interrupt the fantasy. But know this; whatever you're imagining right now, the reality is going to be a thousand times better."

"Promise?" she asked.

"Promise." He covered her mouth with his, their tongues tasting, teasing, exploring. Every nerve lit with electricity, and when thunder rolled overhead, she was half certain they'd caused the commotion.

Christoph's hands were everywhere, in her hair, caressing her neck, her breasts. Hers worked their way down to cup his ass, pulling him so close that his hard length was pressed up against her center. She let out a soft moan as pleasure darted through her.

"You feel so good, Felicia, but I'm going to take my time. You have no idea how much I want to explore every inch of you."

"I don't know if I can wait that long," she said, her fingers trembling as she worked her hand up his shirt and over his rock hard abs.

"Don't you worry about a thing, my little witch. Bringing you pleasure is my only goal." He dipped her backward and scraped his fangs down her neck, sending shivers of delicious desire to all the right places.

"Yes, please."

He chuckled and slipped her T-shirt over her head and tossed it onto the porch. The cool night air tingled over her skin as his tongue darted over the swell of her breast. She arched into him, and a moment later, he undid her bra and cupped her with one hand. His mouth was back on her, his tongue licking, his fangs scraping, and his lips sucking.

Her world fell away, and the only thing she knew was his mouth on her nipple, stroking, pinching, teasing. Then he bit down harder, his fangs ready to pierce her skin. He paused and whispered, "Do you trust me?"

"Yes," she breathed, throwing her head back, ready for all he had to give.

He let out a little growl and clamped his teeth down, piercing the skin on either side of her nipple. His lips pulled her in, and he started to suck.

Intense pleasure exploded, rippling straight to her core, and she grabbed onto his head, holding him in place as she cried out her approval. Her legs came up and tightened around him, her hips pressing into him, as he pressed her back against the porch railing. Her blood surged and pulsed, driving her wild with need.

"More," she demanded.

At the sound of her voice, he sucked harder and just like that, her body tensed and an orgasm slammed into her. She heard the thunder roll and barely felt the fat raindrops that started to fall over her bare chest as the familiar wave took her with so much force she nearly blacked out. Her breath came in ragged gasps as pleasure consumed every part of her.

Christoph retracted his fangs, but continued to suck and tease her nipple until finally she stilled and her breathing started to return to normal. He kissed his way back up to her lips and when her mouth met his, he tasted of warmth and sunshine.

"I'm still going to deflower you," he said, his hands reaching for the button of her jeans.

She gave him a lazy smile. "Right here, in the rain and mud?"

He glanced around as if just noticing that they were still outside and that it had started to rain. "Right. Inside?"

She nodded.

He picked her up, strode across the porch, and was pleased to find the door was already unlocked. Once they were inside, he didn't stop to ask for direction. He strode straight to the back of the house and into her bedroom.

Winston lifted his head off the bed, watching them curiously.

"Three's a crowd," he said and continued on into her oversized bathroom. As he put her on her feet, he glanced around and whistled. "Nice digs, little witch."

She just nodded. Then she met his eyes and slowly started to pull her jeans off.

His gaze traveled down her body, and without a

word, he removed his shirt, kicked off his shoes, and stripped down to nothing but his boxer briefs.

Felicia grinned. "I made sure to leave my sunflower panties on so I don't deprive you of the pleasure of deflowering me, but what's your excuse?"

"None other than I really want those sweet little hands on me." He took a step forward and cupped both of her breasts this time. He brushed his thumb over the two tiny puncture wounds around her nipple. "I just want to make sure you're okay with what happened out there. These will heal by tomorrow, but—"

She pressed her finger to his lips and said, "Shh. I'm more than okay with what we did outside. I think it may have been fairly obvious."

He let out a self-satisfied chuckle. "Well, in the moment, yes it was."

"Don't worry. I'll tell you if I'm uncomfortable with anything we do."

He sobered. "Good."

"Now," she placed her hands on the waistband of his boxers. "It's time to get rid of these."

"Yes, ma'am." He pulled back just enough to give her room to slide his boxers off.

Once he was fully bare before her, she couldn't help herself. She stood there, staring, taking in every inch of his amazing body. He was long and lean, his torso and abs well defined. But he wasn't perfect. He had a series of scars on one shoulder and another long one on his side. She reached out and traced the jagged scar with two fingers, then kissed her way up his chest until she found his lips again. "I want you," she said.

"You've got me."

She moved her hand down and wrapped it around his long shaft. "I want you inside me."

He sucked in a sharp breath as his eyes darkened with need.

Felicia stroked him and bit down softly on his lower lip.

"Jesus," he muttered. In one swift movement, he had her sunflower panties on the floor and his hands on her ass as he picked her up. A moment later, he had her pressed up against the cool tiles of her shower, the hot water streaming over them. He stared into her eyes and brushed her hair back. "I don't think you're quite ready for me just yet. There's one more thing I plan to do."

"Oh? What's that?"

A wicked grin flashed over his face. Then he kneeled before her and ran one hand up her thigh.

She quivered with anticipation.

"Remember that fantasy you had earlier?" he asked as he placed one of her legs over his shoulder.

"Yes," she whispered, praying her muscles wouldn't give out on her.

He pressed a soft kiss to her mound, then moved to the inside of her knee and worked his way up, up, up. Then his breath was on her, blowing into her center.

She buried her hands in his hair, silently begging for more.

"Is this what you wanted, love?" he asked and blew against her again.

It was delicious, made her tremble with anticipation, but she shook her head.

"This?" He pressed his palm to her, cupping her sex.

"Oh... um, no, not exactly."

"Maybe this?" His thumb brushed softly against her already throbbing clit.

Her breath whooshed out of her, and still she shook her head.

He chuckled again and ran a slow finger through her slick heat. Her hips jerked, and she bit down hard on her lower lip. But then his hand was gone and his mouth was on her, his stubbled jaw prickling the inside of her thigh, and she thought she'd die of pleasure right then and there.

"Yes!" she cried, pressing one hand against the wall, while she fisted his hair with the other. "Oh, Christoph, yes, yes."

He attacked her clit with determination, licking, kissing, exploring, then he wrapped his lips around her and sucked, hard.

She shattered. Her entire body trembled and pulsed as lights exploded behind her eyes. She was completely lost, caught up in yet another perfect orgasm. But then Christoph was on his feet, holding her up, wrapping her legs around his waist.

His lips crashed onto hers. He tasted of salt and sex and pure desire. "Ready for me?" he asked.

Unable to speak, she just nodded.

He plunged into her. Her legs tightened around his waist as his hips thrust hard and deep. She dug her nails into his back, holding on as he thrust over and over and over again, until finally he let out a groan and sank his teeth into her neck.

Her world tilted as his bite suddenly pulled the orgasm from deep inside her. Her body tightened around him, and with one last thrust of his hips, they both cried out and got lost in a wave of pure pleasure.

CHAPTER 14

Felicia sat at a table in the back of the tent, watching as the bride and groom waltzed around the dance floor. She'd been dead on her feet when she'd finally made her way into the shop to finish the flowers. After their tryst in the shower, she and Christoph had found their way to her bed where they'd stayed until well past noon the next day.

In fact, it's where she'd left him when she'd finally found the energy to crawl into work. He'd been dead to the world, finally taken down by the daylight.

She'd spent the day in her backroom assembling centerpieces, waiting for Christoph to stop by before the wedding. Early this morning, he'd told her he couldn't wait until the wedding to see her, so she'd told him to visit her at the shop. But as the day wore on and it became that much closer to go time, it became clear he wasn't going to make it. He hadn't even called.

She told herself it was fine. He was the best man, and she knew better than anyone how crazy wedding days could be. She was sure he'd just gotten caught up in last minute details. It wasn't like she wouldn't see him. She had to drop off the rest of the flowers at the wedding venue, after all.

But when she'd gotten there, he was nowhere to be found. He wasn't with Jasper and the other groomsmen when she'd delivered their boutonnieres. Nor had he been anywhere near the bridal suite. She could've asked after him, but she didn't want to bother anyone while they were getting ready for the big moment. So she'd left, taken the remaining flowers to the clearing where the ceremony would be held, and then headed to the reception hall without talking to anyone else.

Now, she was sitting at a table in the back, drinking a glass of non-spelled champagne and wondering when Christoph was going to acknowledge her. She'd finally spotted him taking his seat next to Bianca after all the pictures were taken. Then she'd waited through the dinner and the toasts, trying not to burn holes through his head from staring too much.

The previous night had been nothing short of spectacular, and the fact that he still hadn't even made eye-contact with her was making her doubt herself. Was she fooling herself? Had she only been a fun one-night stand? Was he blowing her off? Her stomach turned and she put the champagne glass down again.

She glanced around, knowing that her job was done. There was no reason to stay. One of the shop assistants could pick up their displays later in the evening. It was time for her to gracefully step out of the picture. The curse Esmerelda had cast might've been neutralized, but that didn't guarantee that Christoph was interested in a relationship with her. Only that it was possible. And judging by the way he appeared to be blowing her off, it was time for her to go.

Felicia grabbed her small handbag and stood.

A large hand landed on her shoulder, and the voice she'd been longing to hear all evening said, "You can't leave yet, little witch. You still owe me that dance."

She turned, and her breath caught at how handsome he was in his tux. She'd known he looked good, but up close and personal, all dressed up, the man was simply irresistible. How was she supposed to walk away from him now? She stared Christoph in the eye and raised one eyebrow. "I was starting to think your dance card was full."

He shook his head, grabbed her hand, and pulled her out onto the dancefloor. "I was saving the last one for you."

"Is that so? Could've fooled me," she said coolly, but she still reached up and wrapped her arms around his neck.

His lips twitched with amusement. "You're irritated. Why?"

She glanced away, suddenly feeling foolish. It wasn't as if she had a hold on this man. They certainly weren't dating. They'd just had one night together. And it was the wedding of his brother and his best friend. Of course he wasn't going to spend all night fawning all over her. She forced a smile. "It's nothing. Never mind."

"It's something," he said, frowning. "Is it because I didn't get a chance to come by the shop today? I can explain—"

She raised a hand cutting him off. "You don't owe me any explanations. Honestly. It's okay, Christoph."

"Sure I do. I said I'd come by and I didn't." He tightened his arms around her waist and pulled her in closer. "Don't you want to know what I was doing?"

Did she? She had no idea. But since he was offering, she nodded. "What were you doing this evening before the wedding?"

He reached into his pocket and pulled out a silver key. "I was signing the paperwork on a rental. Looks like you're going to have a new resident here on Witch Island."

She froze as her mouth dropped open. Then she blinked and said, "What?"

He smiled down at her gently. "One weekend isn't going to be nearly enough for me, Felicia. And I don't mind admitting that I'm not at all ready to leave you or Winston just yet." He winked. "And since it's relatively easy for me to telecommute, I've decided to stay here for a while. I've got an apartment in town with a stunning view of the ocean. Want to see it?"

"When?" she asked, hardly able to process what he was telling her.

"Now."

"Now? We can't go now. It's your brother's wedding."

He laughed. "I've done everything my best man duties require me to do. Now I'm all yours for as long as you'll have me."

She gazed up at him in awe. "You're crazy, you know that?"

"Maybe." His gaze softened as he brought his hand up and cupped her cheek. "But when I want something, I go after it. Is that going to be a problem for you?"

Her mouth worked as she tried to formulate a response. Finally, she narrowed her eyes and pierced him with her stare. There was something she had to know. "I don't get this. If you're sticking around town because you want to get to know me better, then why did you ignore me all night? I mean, you didn't even look at me."

Realization dawned in his steel-blue gaze. "So that's it. Now we're getting to it. That's why you were irritated."

"Yeah. That's why. I was starting to think I was just a one-night stand."

His mirth fled as his expression turned serious. "That couldn't be further from the truth." He held up they key again, proving his point. "I was ignoring you because the only thing I wanted to do all night was ditch Bianca and my brother, grab you, and haul you off to the coat closet, or the limo, or hell even just a dark corner where we could be alone."

Felicia felt all her angst vanish as she beamed at him. "Really?"

"Really. Just do me a favor, okay?"

"What's that?"

He glanced over her shoulder at the bride and groom, then back at her. "Promise me you won't get jealous over my relationship with Bianca."

She frowned. "Why would I do that?"

"Because she's my best friend and we're close."

"Okay, how close? I mean, do you two sleep in the same bed or something? Behave like kissing cousins? Because if so, that might be a little out of my comfort zone."

He threw his head back and laughed. "God no. Nothing like that. We just... talk a lot. And she's the person who knows me best. She's my *person*, for a lack of a better word. In the past, it's been a problem. I don't want it to be a problem with us."

She pressed a hand to his stubbled cheek. "You don't have to worry about that. Just as long as you understand that Chad and I are the same way."

"I do." He bent down and pressed a soft kiss to her lips. "And that answer, little witch, is why I'm pretty damn sure I'm going to marry you some day."

Her eyes widened as she gazed up at him. Then she smiled. "You're getting a little ahead of yourself there, aren't you, cowboy?"

"Maybe. But I just wanted to give you a fair warning."

Happiness burst through her, and Felicia couldn't

remember ever feeling so much joy. She lifted herself up onto her tiptoes and leaned in to whisper, "Consider me warned."

Heat flashed in his steel-blue eyes as he folded her in his arms, bent her back, and with the entire wedding party watching on, he kissed her senseless.

CHAPTER 15

NINE MONTHS LATER

*F*elicia stepped out of the dressing room and smoothed her dress. "How do I look?"

Mystia wiped a single tear from her cheek and nodded her approval. "Gorgeous. Christoph is going to lose his mind."

"Goddess, I hope not," Felicia said with a nervous giggle. "Let's hope he keeps it long enough to get through this ceremony."

"If he's made it this far, I don't think anything is going to scare him off." Mystia handed her the bouquet of roses and adjusted her veil. "Now come on. Let's get out there before the snow starts up again."

Felicia followed her bridesmaid out of the dressing room and grinned when she spotted Chad waiting for her. He let out a gasp, clasped his hand over his mouth, and shook his head, clearly unable to form words.

She slipped her arm through his and held on tight. "Thank you."

"For what," he finally forced out.

"For loving me so much you can't even speak." She leaned over and kissed him on his cheek.

He tightened his hold on her arm. "I do love you, you know."

She nodded, scanned him from head to toe, taking in his perfectly cut tuxedo and freshly cut hair. "Damn you're handsome. I don't know how you're going to top this look for your own wedding next week, but I can't wait to find out."

"Girl, I'm going to be fierce." He winked and added, "And so are you. You should see the dress Jonathon picked out for you."

She chuckled, having finally come to terms with the fact she had no say in whatever she was supposed to wear to their New Year's Eve wedding. Chad and Jonathon were touting it as the party of the year, and even though she and Christoph were supposed to be on their honeymoon, they were coming back early just to help them celebrate. It was an event neither of them were prepared to miss.

The music started, and Mystia waved just before she started down the snow-covered aisle. Their wedding was being held in the island's magical clearing, where the wind was held at bay by powerful spells. There was a babbling brook on one side and a magical winter garden on the other. And the entire area overlooked the dark, churning sea. It was dramatic and romantic, and the perfect place for her to marry her gorgeous vampire.

"It's time," Chad said. "Ready?"

"Absolutely." She took a deep breath and stepped out into the clearing. Her eyes instantly found Christoph. He was standing at the wedding arch, his face lit up with joy. Bianca was beside him, looking as lovely as ever in a red velvet dress. And beside her, Winston, dressed in a wedding vest and bowtie, sat perfectly still, waiting for his mistress to marry the only man who'd ever won over his heart.

"Everyone is beautiful," she whispered to Chad.

"Not as beautiful as you, lovely girl," he whispered back.

She gave him a soft smile, and then turned her attention back to Christoph, hardly able to keep herself from sprinting to his side.

But soon enough, he was holding his hand out to her as Chad took his place as her best man beside Mystia.

Christoph's smile widened as he leaned in and said, "I thought for sure you were going to carry sunflowers."

She glanced down at her red roses and laughed. "I saved those for the wedding night. I figured you'd want to deflower your bride… again."

His hungry gaze traveled down the length of her body. "Please tell me you're wearing them right now."

"I am."

"Thank the gods."

Jasper cleared his throat. "If you two are ready, maybe we could get started."

They both turned their attention to Christoph's brother and nodded.

"Good. Dearly beloved…" he started.

Felicia grinned at her groom and mouthed, *I love you*.

He squeezed her hands and mouthed back, *Forever*.

DEANNA'S BOOK LIST

Pyper Rayne Novels:
Spirits, Stilettos, and a Silver Bustier
Spirits, Rock Stars, and a Midnight Chocolate Bar
Spirits, Beignets, and a Bayou Biker Gang
Spirits, Diamonds, and a Drive-thru Daiquiri Stand

Jade Calhoun Novels:
Haunted on Bourbon Street
Witches of Bourbon Street
Demons of Bourbon Street
Angels of Bourbon Street
Shadows of Bourbon Street
Incubus of Bourbon Street
Bewitched on Bourbon Street
Hexed on Bourbon Street

Last Witch Standing Novels:
Soulless at Sunset

Crescent City Fae Novels:
Influential Magic
Irresistible Magic
Intoxicating Magic

Witches of Keating Hollow Novels:
Soul of the Witch
Heart of the Witch

Witch Island Brides:
The Vampire's Last Dance
The Wolf's New Year Bride
The Warlock's Enchanted Kiss
The Shifter's First Bite

Destiny Novels:
Defining Destiny
Accepting Fate

ABOUT THE AUTHOR

New York Times and USA Today bestselling author, Deanna Chase, is a native Californian, transplanted to the slower paced lifestyle of southeastern Louisiana. When she isn't writing, she is often goofing off with her husband in New Orleans or playing with her two shih tzu dogs. For more information and updates on newest releases visit her website at deannachase.com.

Made in United States
North Haven, CT
16 October 2023